About Time

and other stories

About Time

and other stories

M. Amelia Eikli

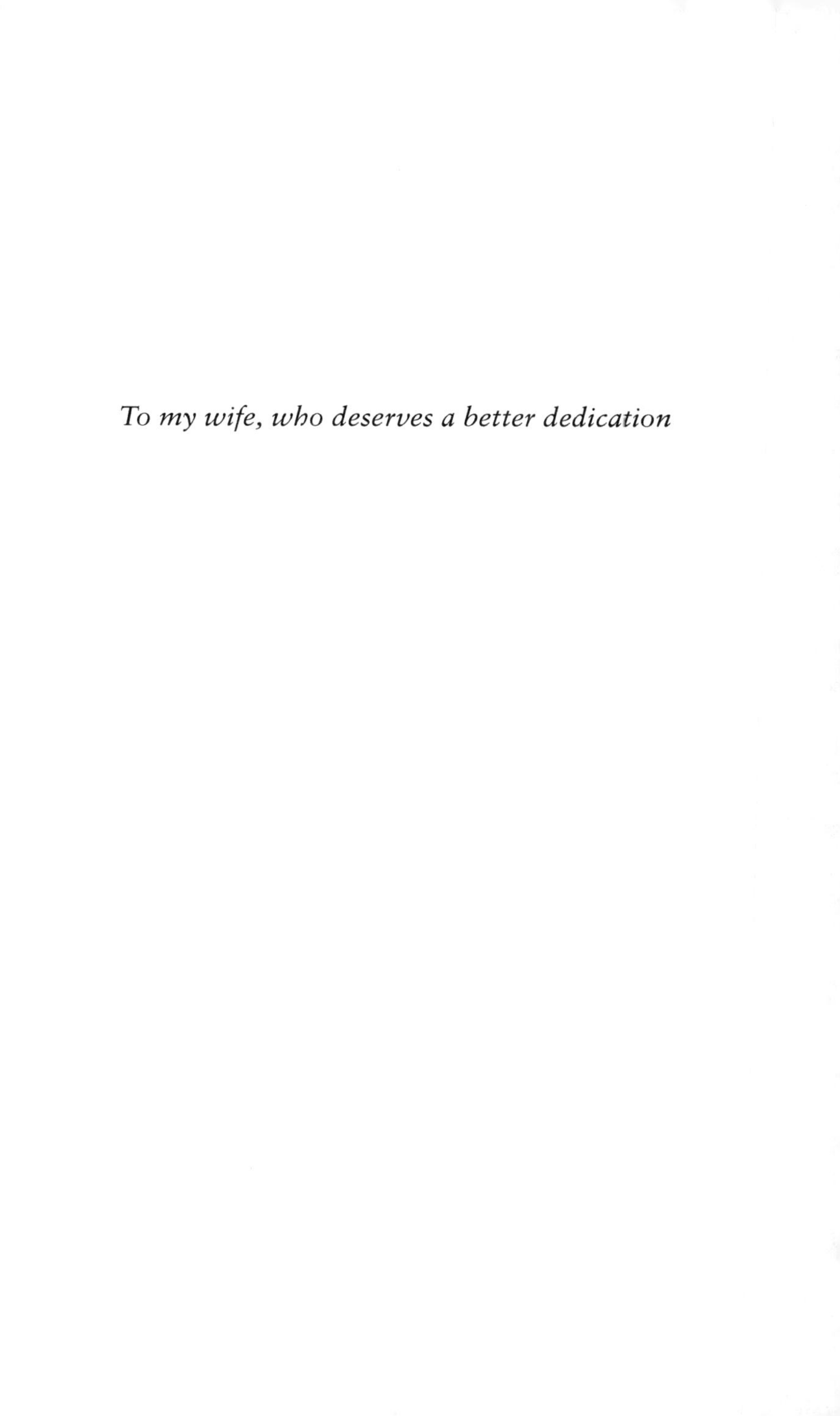

To my wife, who deserves a better dedication

Contents

We Are Out Here   9

In Memoriam   22

Mister *Suffering Misunderstood Artist*   41

Those Who Grow up in Summer   61

About Time   70

We Are Out Here

Two nights before his 80th birthday, my grandfather stole an aeroplane from the Magistrate's Museum and flew out over the sea. He left everything behind except a few clothes and the collection of antiques he had hidden under the floorboards – a brass spyglass and some crumpled maps. The next night, the demolishers came to collect him for the recycling plant and questioned us for hours. How had he managed to get the plane working? How did he know how to fly? Did he know anyone in the museum? Was he part of an anti-demolishment group? And – what interested them more than anything – what had he meant by his note?

The note puzzled my father too. 'They're out there,' it said, and nothing else.

"I don't know!" my father shouted. "Maybe he'd started imagining ghosts, or maybe he was talking about you lot with your organ grinders and poison chambers –" The taller demolisher struck him across the face, "– or maybe he was just an old man with peculiar ideas. He's never talked about resisting demolishment before; we had the funeral only last week and he said he was prepared for the end. I don't know where he is or what he's talking about!"

They tore Grandad's room to shreds and found nothing they shouldn't, so they wrecked the rest of our home as well. They found the painting – 50-credit fine and five lashes for my mum, who tried to stop them taking it – and the radio – 600-credit fine and bitter tears – but they didn't find the five books sewn into our mattresses, or the violin and sheet music hidden in the rehydrator. When they stomped out, the shields of all our neighbouring containers flickered, as worried families wondered if they'd be next.

"You'll have to pay for the plane," the demolishing captain said as they left. "We'll be in touch."

My father cried at the table.

"He's always been selfish," he said, "but this is low, even for him. How are we going to pay for a plane? They just emptied our credits to cover the fines, and a plane from the Before... that's got to be... what? 10,000 credits? 20?"

"Hope," my mum said, "do you know what the note means?" She looked at me. "I think you know what the note means."

I kept sweeping up broken clay from the floor. My prudence bonnet gnawed against my cheek. I was hot, uncomfortable, angry.

"Hope," my father said. "What do you know? Tell me at once."

"No, Sir."

"Hope!" my father said, standing up with a suitably loud bang of his chair. He pushed pen and paper across the table. "You tell me right now." He slapped his hands together.

"Owww!" I cried, scribbling on the pad. "It was ghosts, like you said. He started seeing Grandma and Uncle Eddie last week. He thinks they're out there. In the ocean. I'm sorry I didn't tell you, Father."

"Five lashes," he said. The sound of the whip was earsplitting. I groaned at the first two, then cried and screamed for the last three. Afterwards, I sobbed quietly for a good ten minutes before my mum started comforting me.

"There, there," she said, running some water, dabbing a wet sponge against the table. We smiled at each other.

'The islands,' I had written on the pad. 'He's gone to find the islands.'

They kept the surveillance going for a full month. They think that down in the stacked towns we can't tell when they're listening, but the faint buzz reverberates through our metallic walls, a constant hum. 30 days later, it disappeared. By then, the new tenant had moved in.

Her name was Apina, and she wore a prudence bonnet even though she was at least 40. She never said, but we suspected she was one of the unconnected, the women with no family and no spawn. They were often sent to the outcrops as a last resort, presented to the men of the clean-up crews. Apparently, she'd had no takers, so here she was. She spent most of her time in my grandfather's room when she wasn't at work. She had been placed in one of the assembly lines down the production district and sometimes, she brought home stale bread and left it on the counter. It was a nice gesture, but we didn't dare touch it. We didn't trust her, and she didn't trust us. Meals were a rather subdued affair.

We were having dinner when the buzz finally went quiet, and relief travelled around the table like a wave.

"Thank goodness," said Apina. "You don't notice how loud it is until it's gone."

I exchanged a glance with Mum and Dad, and Dad finally nodded.

"Yes," he said. "We're not big fans either…"

"I'm a friend of Hanneke's," she said. "She said I could trust you…"

There was a tension to this. A static moment in which she had put herself out on the line. We waited. She held her hand up. We waited. She held up three fingers. We waited.

"Freedom, equality, community," she said. "I'm sister Apina, and I reject the Magistrate." Here it was. The second we would throw ourselves over her like wolves, tear her apart, turn her in, watch her burn for heresy, or commit her crime and stand equal.

"Freedom, equality, community," said my mum.

"We are the Owenses, and we reject the Magistrate," said my father. I held up my fingers too. Nodded. She sighed in relief and tore off her prudence bonnet. I looked to Mum, who nodded.

"Good, sweet relief," I moaned as I tore mine off too. This was the longest I had worn my bonnet since the last time we'd had another tenant. But Uncle Eddie – who wasn't really my uncle – had only taken three days to reveal himself as resistance. Tired, exhausted and defiant, he'd thought it would be better to just get it over with and face the consequences. Wearing my bonnet for a full month had, at times, made me so claustrophobic

I cried.

"We are sorry for the long wait, sister Apina," my father said. "Had we known you were resistance, we would have made you more comfortable."

"Not at all," she said, shaking out her frizzy curls. "I was impressed. If I hadn't already known, I would never have suspected. I swear I was even nervous now, coming out, even though Hanneke swore you were trustworthy, you know, but you can't really trust anyone these days. Although, haha, if you were to trust anyone, it would be Hanneke, wouldn't it?" And so it went. The month of quiet co-existence seemed to have bottled up an avalanche of chatter in her body, and from then on, there wasn't a quiet moment at any meal. For weeks, each evening was a constant, rolling deluge of words. But we didn't mind. Apina had information. She knew that the resistance was building a base out at the outcrops, and that they had people on the inside of the recycling plant.

"It's horrible," she said, "it's nothing like they promised. The second someone's clock ticks to 80 years, they're stripped apart, their organs harvested and measured for quality. And the machines... they connect before they rip, so the poor people... They stay alive for up to a minute as they're torn to shreds. They say it's humane..."

She told us colourful stories of hearts scissored out of chests while still beating, eyes scooped out of their sockets being the last thing our 80 year olds saw. Each detail printed itself in my mind, repeated, sputtered, gurgled with blood. I was nauseous.

"...all to ensure optimum quality of organ recycling. But we all know those organs never end up down here in productions, the outcrops or docks. No one in the stacking cities has had a transplant for decades. They all go to the financial districts and high rises. And for that, our old are shredded. And you know what else?" she started, not giving us a second to digest any of this horrid information. It wasn't really news – the rumours of the atrocities going on at the recycling plants had been travelling around for years – but it was something else to have them confirmed.

"So, anyway," Apina said, perhaps finally picking up on the vibe in the room, "have you heard from him?" We all blinked. Somehow, the conversation had dropped us all off at a remote sideway with no way of knowing where we were.

"I'm sorry, heard from whom?" my father said.

"The Pilot?"

"Granddad?"

"Yes, have you heard from him?"

"Surely... he flew straight out over the ocean. We assume he's dead at the bottom somewhere by now. Where would he go?" My father's face had gone dark. Apina looked between each of us, surprised.

"To the islands," she said. "He was going to the islands!" We had questions, many more questions, but then we heard it. The cold metal-against-metal shriek. It sounded innocent, someone replacing a water barrel or closing a storefront, but we all knew it meant incoming controllers. I had gotten too relaxed. My prudence bonnet was under my bed. Mum and Dad moved like dancers through the room, hiding the excess, extinguishing the extra candle, pulling on their aprons and making sure the rehydrator was completely sealed.

Apina tucked her hair into her prudence bonnet, tied her apron tight and that was it – the meek, quiet unnconected that had haunted our house for a month was suddenly back. No spark in her eye. No trace of those large words and endless soliloquies. She was amazing.

A far more terrifying sound thundered through the stacked town. The assembly horn. We lined up in front of our door and waited for the automatic release, then marched along with the rest of the building to the grand square. When we saw the stakes, my stomach dropped. I hated the executions. They were more frequent now. Growing up, I'd only have to watch one or two a year. Now, there seemed to be one a month, at least.

There were 6,000 inhabitants in this district, each of us now orderly stepping in time, shoulder to shoulder in long rows, the system so tightly followed that our address was a perfect map to our location in the square.

Four people were led onto the scaffold, their heads covered in thick hoods. The massive broadcasting screens revealed four beaten faces as the hoods were torn off. I knew all of them, a little. Two of them had worked with my grandfather, the woman for the postal service; the young boy had been in my history class. When the woman's face was uncovered, I felt Apina tense beside me. Anxiousness vibrated through her body. Perhaps she wasn't unnconected after all.

The sentences were read out: heresy, heresy, treason, heresy. As the prisoners were led to the stakes, Apina turned to me, looked me straight in the eye and said, "They're out there." As soon as she said it, she had turned back to the scaffold.

"We the people condemn you," hollered the Magistrate's caller. "Hail the Magistrate!"

"Hail the Magistrate!" we called. The thunderous roar of our voices echoed from the buildings around us.

"Hail the Magistrate!"

"FREEDOM!" someone called.

"Hail the Magistrate!"

"EQUALITY!"

"Hail the Magistrate!"

"COMMUNITY!"

I had gone absolutely cold. Apina was among the callers. There were many. Many hundred voices. Some of the controllers were marching down the rows, trying to find the culprits.

"Hail the Magistrate!" called an ever more uncertain crowd.

"FREEDOM!" There were more now.

"Hail the Magistrate!" I whispered, aware of a controller approaching from my right.

"EQUALITY!" I heard Apina's voice.

"Hail the Magistrate!" I swallowed.

"COMMUNITY!" And this time, I heard my father's voice as well. Hundreds more voices had added to the roar and suddenly, people were moving, splitting through their ranks, going for the stage. The four prisoners were lifted off, the caller and executioner beaten. Controllers blew their whistles, waved their batons, but the throng of people, which had seemed to separate like water for the resistance, was now an impenetrable wall.

I followed Apina's head and grabbed my father's hand as one of the controllers pushed her to the ground. People screamed. The sirens howled. The resistance gathered as many of their people as they could and stormed off down the north line, where three large trucks awaited. The rest of us just stood like cattle in the square. I thought I saw Apina's hair on board a truck. It may have been wishful thinking.

We were in complete lockdown. Anyone who left their house risked being shot. We had no news, no food, no work to go to. The buzz and hum of surveillance rang across the entire town. None of us took our aprons off or loosened our prudence bonnets for days.

On the fifth day, there was a brief knock on the door. Just one short knock, then nothing. We waited for an hour then blew out our candle, and Dad opened the door. There was a small parcel out there. Dad looked around carefully and brought it inside before easing the door shut as quietly as possible. We waited another hour before relighting the candle. No suspicious sounds. No suspicious flickers.

The parcel held a large orange globe. My mum gasped when she saw it.

"It's an orange," she scrawled on the notepad. I wrote back a question mark. The thing was orange, for sure, exciting in itself in this grey, abysmal town, but an orange what? She smiled and picked it up from the little box, held it to her nose and inhaled deeply. My father grinned. A small piece of card had fallen out and

I held it up for them to see.

'They're out here,' it said. It was my grandfather's handwriting. My mum dug her nails into the globe and pulled its thick outer layer off. Inside was something soft and watery. She broke off a piece and put it in my mouth. Sweet. Sour. Fresh. There were words in this flavour I hadn't understood before. My parents watched as tears welled up in my eyes, then cried with me as they ate their pieces.

Eventually, things went back to normal. More or less. We didn't get another tenant, and neither did many of the neighbours who had been housing members of the resistance – without their knowledge, of course. The hum of the constant listening stuck around the whole season, and when it finally died down one day in July, it struck me like physical relief. Seconds later, there was a knock at our door. A few moments passed, then some-one knocked again. Was someone actually standing on our doorstep, knocking? Someone who – in broad daylight – wanted to come in?

As soon as Dad touched the handle, the door flew open and Apina sprung inside, shutting it again behind her.

"We don't have long," she said, her cheeks red and puffy. "Get everything you need ready for 22:48. You'll hear a click, then just exit the door, go straight to the square. He'll be waiting. Do you understand?"

"No," my dad said, but Apina waved him off.

"Just do what I said. It is the only way." She smiled at me. "He's out there," she said, then hurried back out through the door. Mere moments later, the buzzing came back. The resistance was getting stronger. They had managed to cut the surveillance. The Magistrate's men wouldn't like that.

At 22:47, we were stood by the door. We hadn't packed much. The books, some clothes, the violin, the notepad and pen. Mum was nervous, Dad was anxious, I was excited and terrified. What were we doing? Why were we doing it? A loud click resonated through the containers and our door sprung open, just like that. The town was in complete darkness.

"Hold on," my father said, placing my hand in Mum's and her other in his. Quickly, we scurried through the street towards the square, knowing we would be punished if anyone saw us. Apina joined us from a side street.

"Do you hear it?" she whispered. At first I didn't, but slowly my ears picked up the loud engine sound drawing closer.

"We'll only have a few moments," Apina said, picking up speed. "Hurry! As soon as he's slowed down enough, we have to jump."

The plane was much smaller than I had imagined, and when it started its descent onto the plaza, I realised this plan was not only dangerous, but also terrifyingly difficult. We stood by the central scaffold and the plane came in from the north. The plaza was big, but we'd have to time our run perfectly as it slowed down and rolled across the smooth stones.

"Go!" Apina called, just as the plane touched ground. We ran. I ran the fastest I'd ever run. My mum ran, my father ran. Our timing was off, but we pushed harder. My father tossed our large bag inside then jumped, caught the door, was pulled inside by strong arms. Apina jumped, timed it perfectly, dove through the open hole. Mum jumped, as gracious as a cat, but I could feel myself falling behind.

Come on, I told myself. *It's now or never.*

"Jump!" a man in the door yelled. "We have to speed up again NOW! Jump!"

The plane accelerated and I was still running.

"Jump!" my father called.

"Jump!" my mother called.

"Jump, goddamn it, JUMP!" called Apina. I leapt through the air. Hit the side of the plane, was propelled backwards but managed to grab on to the door with the tips of my fingers. The plane still accelerating, I felt I was trailing out in the free air. The man I had seen in the doorway stepped out onto a small ledge and wrapped his arm around my wrist, holding on to a strap inside. My father leaned out, grabbed my other hand, I kicked against the side of the plane, and they hauled me inside just as the wheels left the ground.

We're too close to the houses, I thought. *We're going to crash... we're too close to the houses.*

"Hahaaaaaaaaa!" came the familiar laughter of my grandfather. "I didn't think we'd make that one."

My stomach turned as we tilted in the air, and then we were above the town. Then I saw the lights from the city. Then I saw the ocean glittering below.

"What's happening down there?" I said, seeing blazing flames from the docks.

"The resistance," Apina said, pointing to a trail of boats and ships out at sea, sailing in the same direction we were flying.

"Where are we going?"

"The islands."

I looked back at the lights from the city. Thought about all the families we had left behind in the stacks. Families that would now, undoubtedly, go through another lockdown. More days of uncertainties and punishments. Then I looked out to the sea and thought of oranges. I wondered what unfiltered sunshine would feel like on my skin.

The resistance radio broadcasted from the islands every evening for one hour. The time and frequency changed, the code of calculation freely available to those who knew someone who knew someone.

"Remember," Apina said, as my mum started playing a song on her violin. "No matter how hopeless it all feels, no matter how far away our ideals seem, nothing is lost. Freedom, equality and community will be yours. All you have to do is resist. And remember," she said, my mum's playing building to a crescendo.

"We are out here."

In Memoriam

The doctor waved his arms about, angrily punctuating his sentences with slashes and dashes. The door was shut and the glass thick, but that just made it worse. Every time the air cycle started, the vents between the operating theatre and them opened for a split second, allowing single words to seep through. Not enough to understand. But enough to know something was seriously wrong.

"IMPOSSIBLE ... RESPONSIBLE ... DEAD! ... HOW ... ... TIME ... LEGAL!"

The technician kept running his hands through his hair, quite literally clutching at straws, I thought. He shook his head, pulled his hair, but didn't say much. The sales rep looked like she was going to faint. She kept looking in at me, my head still cracked open like a breakfast egg, and her cheeks bulged with the effort not to vomit there and then. I wasn't too worried, not really, until the lawyer came in. His eyes were hard, and when he caught mine through the glass, he hurried to draw the curtains.

It was only the doctor who yelled. The lawyer, whatever he was saying, was making the doctor more upset.

"DAMAGE CONTROL ... TIME? ... ... MY WORK! ... ... MEMORIES ... SOLUTION!"

"NEVER!"

I closed my eyes and tried not to focus on the truth that kept screaming for attention.

Think of something else, I told myself, but that came too close to the truth too. *There's nothing to think about. There is absolutely nothing to think about.* A nervous-looking nurse came in to check my vitals. She smiled what I'm sure she thought was a reassuring smile, and I smiled back, so she wouldn't feel bad.

"Guess they're pretty nervous out there," I said as more words seeped through the vent. Her eyes darted from the vent to me, from the drawn curtains to the floor.

"They're just trying to figure out the best course of action," she said. "You just try to relax." She moved in behind me. Every now and then, I caught a glimpse of her in the mirror the doc had used to keep an eye on me during the operation, but most of the time I could just hear the light shuffling of her feet.

"Am I dying?" I said after a while.

"No," she said, "you're not dying. Well..." she said, considering the truth of her statement. "No, you're not dying."

"But something is very wrong?"

"Just give it a few more minutes," she said, patting my shoulder gently as she passed. "I'm sure they'll be back in a flash to explain it all."

"Hey, nurse?" I said as she reached the door. "What's my name?"

She looked uncomfortable, peered down at the form she was clutching. "A. Lock," she said.

"What's the A for?"

"I... I don't know," she said, backing out of the room without looking at me.

She didn't know. I didn't know. And then the beeping began. The doctor, the nurse and a handful of other people came running into the room. Everything suddenly seemed bathed in pink and purple. Their voices were distant and far away.

This is all I remember. All I remember that I know is mine.

"What do you mean?" says the old man at last. He's stopped halfway through patching up my arm, holding the needle in the air as if ready to conduct an orchestra.

"I mean, that's all I remember that's definitely *my* memory. I know it's mine, because I can see my hands in it, and I have this little scar on my finger, right here." I lift my hand to show him. My finger is bruised and swollen like the rest of me, but the scar is still visible – a thin, bright V right under my knuckle. I wish I remembered how I got it.

"I have many memories," I continue. "I remember being five years old on Essux Ex, and also being five years old and dying in a hospital in a different galaxy all together. I remember getting married about a dozen times. I remember so many ships and planets... I don't know how I'd even go about beginning to count them. But I don't know which of them – if any – belong to me."

"Is that so," he says, finally. He continues to sew up the gash. His fingers are old and stiff, but there's a nimbleness to his movements. He's done this before.

"Thing is," he says when he's snipped the thread and bandaged my wound, "There ain't that many ways of gettin' down here accidentally. You must have been dropped here, one way or another. Lucky to have survived the transport, really."

"Yeah," I say, groaning as I try to shuffle myself into a sitting position, "I feel lucky."

Every single part of my body hurts. My right leg's probably broken. The gash on my arm looks like it should have killed me and my skin can best be described as 'bruise-coloured'. Whatever happened to me, it happened to me very hard.

"Now, boy," the man says, and I startle.

"Boy?" I say and look down across my flat chest. "Huh... I could have sworn I was a girl... I... thought I remembered..." I swallow. Take a deep breath. I mustn't panic. That, I know for sure. If I panic, I worry all my memories will be twirled up and I'll forget which one is mine. I'll never find this one again. The one that has my real name: A. Lock.

"I just thought I was a girl," I say, regaining my composure.

"'Fraid not," he says, pulling at his scruffy beard. I can't put my finger on why, but knowing I'm a boy changes me. I feel my body relaxing a little. Up until now, I've been very aware of my naked body under the thin sheet. On guard. Tense. Now, I feel safer. It's strange. Ridiculous, really. I know nothing of this man or his desires.

"I remember giving birth," I say as the memories of several childbirths come crashing into my head all at once. Some went well, some didn't. Some were easy, some weren't. One, I could have sworn killed me. I remember dying. On the other hand, I remember watching my wife... no, wives, give birth. I remember becoming a father. Eager and reluctant, angry and pleased. I remember knowing the child isn't mine, and I remember seeing myself in its face. Each of the memories is rock solid, and they all hurt like knives in my mind.

I know what being stabbed feels like. I know what it feels like to get shot. I've had the air sucked out of me, being shot out of an airlock. I've been tortured, abused. I've known tremendous joy. Nothing is mine.

I can't fight it any longer. The fear pushes into me from everywhere and draws hope out of my chest in big wet sobs.

"There, there, boy," says the old man. He pats my knee. It hurts like hell, but then again, so does everything. "Pull yourself together know. I think we need to take you to Heddy. She's good with all these augie things."

"Augie things?"

"You know... Augies. Augmentation implants."

I search my memory for any matches. Skim through what feels like hundreds, maybe thousands of lives, looking for the word 'augie'. Nothing.

"I don't know what they are," I say.

He looks puzzled. Perhaps a little amused. "I'll be damned," he says, pulling at his beard again. "Heddy's gonna love hearin' that. Hey... do you think you can walk?"

The angle of my right leg doesn't look right, even to my untrained eye.

"I don't think so," I say.

He sighs. "All right. I'll go get Bessie. I'll be back in

a bit."

I hear a loud FSHHH as he leaves the building. Somewhere in my mind, a bell rings, and I recognise this sound. It feels threatening and it feels like home.

"Airlock," I mumble. "It's just an airlock."

I look around. I woke up in this room, the old man already working on my wounds. I freaked out for about a minute, until he gave me something that made me fall asleep. I slept for a long time.

The room is sparse. A bed and a chair, a communications port, a few tablets and a bunch of old books. A collector, maybe. Or just someone too poor to buy tokens. The needle and thread came from an old-fashioned doctor's bag. The kind they use on the battleships. White and sleek with a high-pressure vacuum inside, allowing them to pack much more than what would normally fit. It's old. This type was banned at least 40 years ago. They kept exploding and scattering fragments of medical equipment everywhere.

It strikes me that I remember this happening. I've seen it, twice. Once, I was a medic and my pack exploded overnight in storage. No one got hurt. We just thought of it as a funny little accident. The other time, I was a young soldier, dying on the mud planes of Terrax-5. A field medic came running towards me, then disappeared in a pop of pink mist. Pieces of cotton and bandages rained over me, then a scalpel fell through the air, quick and shimmering like a falling star. It hit me in my throat. I remember thinking it was an ironic death, to be killed by a field medic trying to save your life.

As I remember these things, I notice other memories trying to force their way through. Some of them are edged with fear, and I don't want to let them anywhere near my consciousness. I'm hiding dark deeds in my mind. I remember taking lives. I remember taking lives in cold blood. I shuffle through some happy memories to pass the time. Memories of proud moments seem to be the strongest. The first time I manned a Hawk Shuttle. The first time I had a token published. When I passed the medical exam. When my son was born.

It's clear to me that these memories aren't all me, yet they all *feel* like me. I have murdered so many people. I have loved so many people. I have fathered so many children, and given birth to just as many. Twice, I come across the same memory from two different perspectives. I see my wife across the room, and love her so fiercely it breaks my heart. And then I see myself, who is my husband, through my own eyes, which belong to my wife, and I know I don't love him anymore.

This will drive me crazy. I push all other memories away and just bring up the one I know belongs to me. I go through it over and over. Try to see if I can remember any names. Any identifying information. Is there something written on the wall behind the nurse? Something hospital, is it? Or am I just plastering in a thousand other memories from a thousand other hospitals, wanting to make this one count? I wish I could go to sleep.

Bessie is a rusty field crosser with a pressurised cargo hold. The old man half carries me out into the airlock and helps me get a pressure suit on.

"Just in case," he explains. His voice sounds clangy and metallic through the helmet. "Bessie's my bestie, but she's old. Don't want to get stranded out there without your suit." He helps strap me into the passenger seat. Some of my memories fire up. Ejector seat – the old kind. Field crosser mechanics. Fuel consumptions. A moment later, I feel like I've known Bessie all her life and am ready to trust her with mine.

She flies smoothly, uses the 20-foot long field rudder to keep her stable. 20 feet is just high enough that I get a good overview of the landscape, but low enough that I'm sure I'd survive a crash. That's good. Her engine sputters and coughs. I look around.

"What is this place?" I shout to reach the old man over the roar of the engines.

"It's a waste planet. Medical, mostly."

"Medical waste? Like... hospital waste?"

"Yeah. One of the tech corps has a spot here too, that's why Heddy's settled here. But we're mostly medical."

"So when you said I had to have been dropped here... you meant..."

"As medical waste. Yeah. Two big hauls came in yesterday. You were in one of 'em."

"Do you know which ship?"

"Nah. The transporters pick up on a rota. May have been combined from four or five different hospital ships. There are loads of 'em in this quadrant due to the wars over that new platinum galaxy."

"At least that's something," I say, more to myself

than to him.

"What?"

"At least I know what quadrant I'm from."

He shrugs, because he doesn't understand. I have memories from every galaxy I can think of. And I can think of so very many galaxies.

There are wide paths dug into the waste. Bessie's rudder skates through one of them towards a cluster of buildings in the distance.

"I certainly couldn't have walked this far!" I shout again, but he shows me the tracks of a small train we'd be on if I could have walked to where they started. I couldn't have. My leg screams at the mere thought.

The buildings hurtle towards us as we hurtle towards them, and soon, he brings Bessie down on her rudder, and we slide into a garage under the domed building in the middle.

"Welcome to the university," he says.

"There's a university here?"

"No. But there used to be."

My ears are still ringing with the sound of Bessie's engine, so it takes me a few moments to catch onto the voice speaking to us through speakers outside.

"...airlock five," it says. "We've had another problem with four. Who's that? Oh shit. Did you find a live one? Holy shit, he's seen better days. All right. I'm coming down."

The old man's eyes smile through his helmet.

"That's Heddy," he says and lifts me up to take me to airlock five. "She's enthusiastic."

"You know what?" I say. "I just realised I don't know

your name."

He chuckles. "Staples. The name's Staples. Pleasure to meet you."

I moan loudly as he drops me in front of the door. "Let me assure you," I say through clenched teeth, "the pleasure is all mine."

Heddy really is enthusiastic. Her curls bounce around her head as she flits this way and that, punching buttons on her big screens.

"Definitely got an augie in there," she says, pointing to a small white square on my head scan. "A D4 or D5, if I'm not mistaken."

"What does that mean?"

"It means you – or someone who liked you a whole lot – had money. The D-series is the best there is."

"What does it do?" I say. And she frowns.

"Yeah, before I tell you, I need to ask you something. Do you really not know what an augie is? In none of your memories?"

I close my eyes and scan my mind one more time. Shuffle through memories of so many faces. Some I miss like a punch to the stomach. Some scare me. I love hundreds and thousands of people. I hate a few. They all talk to me in these memories. Tell me about their day, or about something they need or dream about, or why they dislike me, and a billion other things. But there's no 'augie' anywhere.

"No. I really don't," I say. Heddy and Staples look at each other.

"I told you," she says.

"Yep," he says, nodding. He looks grim.

"Look," I say. "Could one of you tell me what's going on?"

Heddy clicks around on her screen again, then draws up a holo of a robust woman with burning red lips. Every single one of my memories screams out to me at once. I am a thousand voices, all saying the same thing.

"Doctor Elizabeth Mabagambe," I gasp, clutching my head to make the voices go away. "I remember her name. I don't... remember why."

Heddy nods, then a video starts playing.

"I am Doctor Elizabeth Mabagambe," says the video. "And here at MemoEx, we are dedicated to protecting the most precious thing you have: your memories."

She rambles on and on about how fragile brain tissue is. About how storing memories in your brain is old-fashioned and unreliable. As she talks, she walks through white rooms where smiling people hold up whats-its and doo-das to the camera, and beautiful people lie back in big chairs to let doctors plug chips into their brains.

"Your memories will be stored safely in the universal memory cloud storage system, protected and controlled by the strictest privacy protocols ever known," she says. The very idea gives me the creeps. I can see them up there, trillions of memories, floating about, inside fences and shields. "There, your memories are ready for you to access at your convenience – as crisp and clear as when you first experienced them. And, of course, your memories are only accessible through your chip."

A brief animation begins, showing how one chip has

a clear path to a specific golden memory, while the next one doesn't. Hundreds of light trails spread out from hundreds of animated chips, dance across the lady's face as a hologram inside the hologram. *And what if*, I think, *what if they're memories about holograms?*

"…to relive your favourite memories, and share the highlights of your night with friends? Our premium line lets you rewind, delete and share your memories to any social web of your choice, with a simple thought." The woman blinks and on the screen behind her, we see her memory – the camera, and cameramen waving happily as her words repeat themselves. Then she blinks again, and the memory disappears. She looks confused for a split second, then laughs.

"I now forgot having to watch that again," she laughs, then pushes forward.

"And when your life ends," she says, suddenly looking as serious as I am, "with our full life coverage, your memories will be accessible to your loved ones forever. Your grandchildren can see how much you loved them, your great-grandchildren can get to know you through your own memories."

She bends down to hug two small children, so pretty and preened they hardly seem real. I swallow. I miss my children.

"…need for privacy. As part of our service, your memories will be washed by one of our trusted confidentiality partners. Anything too private or unseemly will be locked away. Not only do we care about your memories," the woman says, smiling reassuringly at the camera. "We care about how you are remembered."

The ad closes with a spinning MemoEx logo, then blurs to a stop and disappears.

"That... does not sound like something I'd be interested in," I say, and hear it echo as truth from all my inner voices. Heddy and Staples exchange a glance again.

"Well... The MemoEx market share is at 64% now. There's hardly anyone left who doesn't have any sort of augie at all. Most people just do a simple recorder, of course, but more and more are opting for advanced options. The black market is huge."

"How... Who would let someone put a chip in their brain on the black market?" I ask, the very thought making my stomach churn.

"No, you misunderstand. There's hardly any demand for black-market *chips*. The real money is in black-market memories," Heddy explains. "Memory hacking is, of course, strictly forbidden. But the security systems aren't perfect, especially not if someone consents to sharing their memories. Think about what you could do with other people's memories. Blackmail, torture, even just passing exams, spying on your enemies..."

"Wow," I say.

"Yeah, wow indeed," says Heddy. "Basically, the whole concept is evil and perverted. More and more of us think so. And when memories are stored digitally, they can just be wiped if whatever backwater government you're under thinks they should be. Even a president had his mind wiped when he was no longer trusted with the information he'd gained during office. There are countless examples like that. We're a bit amazed more people aren't refusing to have the chips put in. We both had ours taken out years ago," she says, nodding to Staples, who gives a confirming nod back.

"But they've got some issues up at MemoEx, I think," she continues. "All over, people seem to have forgotten they have the chips. They use their chips, they sign up for new chips, they react positively to the adverts, but they seem unaware that they have them. It's as if the chips exist right outside their memories. It's odd." I agree with her there. "And we've had a few bodies turn up down here with augies still in their brains. Five that we've found, but could be more. On busy days, we don't get to check all the containers before releasing the pressure seal. We just dump them on the surface and get on with our day."

"Thank you for checking mine," I say.

"Was different with you," she shrugs. "Your container had a heat signature."

"Mind you," says Staples, "It's not completely unusual for medical waste to have a heat signature. If there's enough tissue, for example, it may start decomposing before it reaches us. But your signature was very... distinctly human."

"Anyway," Heddy says. "It's weird. Usually, people have their chips removed when they die. They're synced to the dead-cloud then given to the relatives. But you guys, you've still got your chips in place. And it's more than that. You've not been logged as deaths at any hospital I can find. It's all rather mysterious and wonderful!" she says.

I look at the scan in front of me. Look at the little

white square that was meant to hold all my memories, and now is holding other people's.

"Can you fix me?" I ask Heddy.

"I don't know," she says, smiling a little. "But I can try."

I'm tired. For three days, Heddy's been scanning my brain while asking me thousands of questions. She's kept an eye on the radiation levels and the rate of signals going in and out of the chip. Her face has turned darker and her consciousness is somewhere else completely. Whatever she's learning, she doesn't like it. Staples hangs around most of the time. He talks to me when Heddy's too distracted, makes sure my bandages are changed and that we remember to eat.

"So, I have some bad news, some more bad news, and some good news," Heddy says as the third day draws to a close.

"Okay…" I say, tapping nervously on the cast Staples has made for my broken leg. "How about we start with the good?"

"Eh… can't do that," Heddy says, bouncing around, pushing buttons to bring my scans up on the screens around the room. "You won't think it's good unless I tell you the bad first."

"Okay," I say. "Shoot."

"So, the bad news is that you don't exist."

I blink. Then I blink again. "Excuse me?"

"You, A. Lock – the A stands for Arelian, by the way – don't exist. You were born on December 1st 646B on Ax Medum, and you died four days ago in

Pal A Star Hospital ship during a standard operation to upgrade your MemoEx chip. You attended school, graduated with a degree in Philosophy…" She looks at me and rolls her eyes. I can't blame her. No one studies Philosophy anymore. It's a subject for rich, spoiled kids who don't have to worry about the real world. "But that's it," she says. "In no other sense of the word 'exist' do you exist."

"I don't get it," I say.

"Between your birth and your death, and except for the three official papers marking your registration and graduation from each level of school, there is no memory of you. You won't have any, your parents won't have any, your teachers, your friends – no one has a memory of you. Not if, that is, they have some sort of augie. And they all, most likely, do. 98.2 percent of us do."

"I…" I say, but I don't understand enough to have a proper emotional reaction.

"Something happened during the operation. Your chip got connected to the universal memory cloud, then wiped itself from it. Every single memory corresponding with one of yours had your side of it scrubbed. It shouldn't be possible. Heck, I'm sure if you asked MemoEx, they'd insist it isn't possible. But that's what happened. They've made the smallest internal memo on it. No D-series chips are to be upgraded until they've made sure backward surges can't happen."

I know I should be upset. This comes to me the way you remember you're supposed to take your shoes off when you enter someone's cabin, or that you shouldn't burp at the table if you're eating with someone from the Hillax Quadrant. And still, I'm not upset. I can't remember the people who've forgotten me. Heck, I can't even remember who I am to forget.

"Hold on," I say. "That doesn't explain why I have so many other people's memories in my head."

"That... kind of brings us to bad news point two," she says. "You died."

"What?" I say, although I remember dying so many times that it doesn't actually surprise me.

"Twice, actually. You died during the initial backward surge. I think that's how the others died as well. Then you woke up, stayed awake for a few minutes – those are the minutes your chip's surge feature recorded – then died again. Somehow, your chip's non-existent memory was transferred to the dead storage of the cloud, and brought with it a link back. You remember dead people's lives. Loads of them, too, from what I can tell."

"Oh," I say, noticing how every single one of my lines of memory ends at dying. I remember dying over and over. Of age, of heart attacks, while falling, at war. I'm an endless number of lived lives, unfulfilled potential and dreams that came true.

Heddy is pretty, I think. Her broad nose and tight curls remind me of a hundred someones, but her smile is just her own.

"So, what's the good news?" I say.

"No one at the hospital can remember admitting you. Your family insist they've never had a son named Arelian. Everyone thinks you were a computer glitch, and no one knows what to do with computer glitches.

At some point, you were designated as medical waste and sent here. To me." She smiles. "And I'm intensely good at what I do."

"What do you do?"

"This and that. But for the purposes of this conversation, I am really good at giving people new starts. New name? No problem. New documents? Not at all an issue. Just tell me what sort of life you want to live, and I can make it happen."

I look around. Everything is equal parts familiar and strange. There are a thousand things I want to do. Take up flying again, mothering again, find the hundreds of children I know and make sure they're all right. I'm a woman, I'm a man, I'm something else altogether. I'm old and young, good and bad. And the only thing I am – more than all that – is right here, right now, in this bruised and broken body.

"Well," I say. "What sort of life do you live right here?"

"Well…" she says, looking to Staples, who just shrugs.

"Not like he can get away if he objects to it," he says, chewing on the nail of his left index finger. She laughs.

"True. Basically, we're people who accepted jobs at a waste-disposal planet in order to do things… let's say, slightly under the radar. Personally, I'm working on taking down MemoEx, outlawing augies and making sure all memories are returned to brain tissue before the cloud's closed down," she says. She looks at me defiantly. As if challenging me to object to her plan, or call it out for being all the things it truly is.

"Is that all?" I smile. I have no objections. She shrugs.

"Tell you what," I say. "If I help you, can we see if we can restore the existence of A. Lock while we're at it?"

She wrinkles her nose. It's one of the cutest things I've ever seen, in any life, at any time.

"Well…" she says. "I don't think that's possible."

"That's okay. I'd still like us to try, though."

She smiles and turns back to her wall of screens. After a few moments, she seems to forget I'm there.

"Hey, you wouldn't happen to know anything about tissue programming, would you?" she says, as some horribly complicated formulas pop up on the screen to her left.

I close my eyes and scan around, pick up pieces of information from a dozen helpful lines. I smile.

"As a matter of fact," I say, drawing up a chair and hobbling over to her. "I think I wrote the book on it."

I set off to work, slowly learning how to choose what I access and when. I catch a glimpse of my reflection in one of the screens, and I look back in loving memory of myself.

Mister *Suffering Misunderstood Artist*

Day 1.

"Welcome to the Infinite Hotel," says the nurse, and then she laughs the way people laugh in old slapstick movies. She roars, bends forward holding her stomach, slaps her thighs and moves her head slowly from side to side. "HO HO HO!" she says at last, before straightening up and straightening her skirt and straightening her face into a serious, blank plane. Her face is a tundra in snow. Flat. Bare. Cold.

"Good morning," she says, "and welcome to the Infinite Hotel."

"Where am I?" I say. "Who am I? What happened? Where am I?"

Her smile breaks the ground apart and splits the tundra in two. Rubble, ice and frozen mammoths disappear down her widening grin.

"Good morning! Welcome to the Infinite Hotel, Mister *Suffering Misunderstood Artist*," and her face freezes over again. I realise she's not looking at me. She's looking past me. Through me. Her eyes aren't looking at all, they're painted on. A porcelain doll.

"I'm sorry," says a young woman, hobbling in through a door to my left, pulling her trousers on. "That's Miss *Angel Of Mercy*. We don't know exactly what happened to her, but she's been glitching lately. Now she just hangs out in reception and makes people feel they'd be better off dead."

The nurse tilts her head and laughs again. "HA HA HA," she howls, slapping her thighs in sheer amazement. "Well, I've never! Ha HA! Ha HA!"

The other lady pulls her zip up, then shoves her hand into mine. "I'm Miss *Girl Who Pretends To Be One Of The Guys To Get Attention From Boys*," she says, pulling her ponytail out through the back of her cap, and shakes my hand, hard and fast. "Great to meet you." She stops for a second, looks up at me and blinks, her long lashes brushing daintily against her cheeks. She blushes. "Right this way," she says, confident and brusque again.

"I've always suspected girls did that," I say.

She snorts, steps back out through the door and into an absolutely white room. It's nothing but white. I don't know if it's large or small, if it has doors or windows, because every single surface is nothing but white.

"Yeah, no duh. That's why I'm here. Because of guys like you," she says. Rolls her eyes. Hikes her trousers up. Spits.

"What do you mean?" I say.

"Oh, that's right," she says. "You haven't had the tour yet." She fishes a clipboard out from thin air, looks at it for half a moment, then grabs a pen from somewhere right above her head. "Sign here," she says.

"...No?" I say. "I'm sorry, but... I don't even know who you are. What is this place? How did I get here? And... who am I, for that matter?"

She yawns. "Listen, you'll get the tour, and you'll get the answers, but before we can start, I need you to sign this."

I look at her paper. It holds a big logo, 'SOCICON INC', and the text reads, 'I, the signatory, confirm that I have read and understood this contract,' and then there's a space to sign.

"What contract?"

"This contract." She shakes the clipboard.

"A contract to understand a contract? That's all?" She shrugs, and I sign. The clipboard disappears and in the blink of an eye, the walls, floor and ceiling of the room fill in. Flowery wallpaper and hundreds of black and white photographs surround me. There are dark hardwood floors and plaster roses in the ceiling.

"What the…"

"Welcome to the Infinite Hotel," she smiles, stepping through heavy doors in front of us. "This is the reception area. This is where newcomers come in, and this is where you go when it's time to die or be reborn."

"To… what?"

"Over here," she says, pushing open another set of doors, "is the restaurant. Most avatars spend their time in here. There's a buffet; it will have whatever you expect a buffet to have, so… imagine a good one," she says and winks. "Just a little tip for you there, haha – and there are board games and paper and stuff over there." She points to a long row of bookshelves in a corner. The restaurant is crowded, but not cramped.

"Wow… is there some sort of costume-fest going on?"

"No? Oh, yeah. By the way. You're an avatar. Everyone here is an avatar," she says, now holding a baseball bat over her shoulder. She looks relaxed, sexy, strong and fragile. She scares me, so I don't like her.

"Avatar?" I say.

"An avatar is…"

"I know what an avatar is, young lady, I simply mean…"

She rolls her eyes. "See that guy over there?" she says, pointing to a man through the crowd who's talking at two young women. One is heavily bruised and dressed in skimpy clothing, the other has a broad smile and seems eager to agree with the guy. And still… there's a look that passes between them. A look of exasperation perhaps. Of tired resign. "That's Mister *Mansplaining*. Do you maybe know what that is, already?"

"I most certainly do," I say, insulted by the suggestion that I wouldn't. "Coined by Rebecca Solnit, it's the…" Then I see the laughter in her eyes, and I shut up.

"So, take everything you know about that concept, and how it shaped the cultural consciousness in its time. Everything that comes to mind, the personification of that is Mister *Mansplaining*."

"In its time?" I say, "It's only been around for a few years, hasn't it?"

"Well… yes and no. When *you* come from, it has, but in the whole history of the world, it has simultaneously not happened yet, and happened a very long time ago. The Infinite Hotel is infinite."

"What do you mean 'when I come from'?"

"So, you've been picked to serve 100 years as the avatar of *Suffering Misunderstood Artist*, because you were fairly close to encompassing the term when you were alive. And as the Infinite Hotel needs some fixed time points to function properly, we're probably matching up with your timeline right now," she says, smiling apologetically. I huff. I puff. I blow hard through my nose.

"I – but I… Not going to!"

"Hey, listen," she says, smiling, "I wasn't a tomboy to get attention from boys, okay? That's just the idea. That's what people think is true. Sometimes ideas are real, sometimes they're not. We had Miss *The Earth is Flat* here for a long way, but her idea seems to be back in vogue now, in whatever timeline you come from, so she was moved to the Gold Room this morning."

"But I'm not a suffering misunderstood artist," I say.

"Aren't you?" She looks me up and down, so I do too. I look scruffy. A few nights of too much whiskey and not enough sleep. Ink splots on my hands. *Computers just don't feel the same as a good ol' fountain pen.* My stomach is rumbling. *It's not about being able to afford food, Myriam, it's about whether I think food is more important than finishing this book!* I grumble.

"Anyway, your room is on…" She snaps out another clipboard and rummages through the papers until she finds a room for me. "14," she says.

"14? All these people live in this hotel, and I've got room 14?"

She shrugs again. "Breakfast, lunch and dinner are served all day. Enjoy your stay," she says.

"No. I'm not doing this. I'm not going to be some goddamn avatar."

"But you signed the contract," she says, confused.

"What… It… The contract just said that I had read

and understood the contract!"

"Of course that's not *all* it said," she says, now wearing a T-shirt from a really obscure computer game and holding a controller in her hand. "Didn't you read the fine print?"

"What fine print?!" I say. "That's literally all that was on the contract."

She looks around. "Hey," she says, waving someone over, "can you explain the contract?"

"Oh," says the newcomer, "you always have to read the fine print." He picks my contract out of the air and points to the logo in the top-right corner. I squint.

"There is no fine print," I say. They look at each other. They act as if I'm being unreasonable.

"Right there," he says, then sighs, pulls a magnifying glass into existence and hands it to me. "Literally, right there," he says. And I see it now. The logo is made up of teeny tiny words.

Contract between Daniel Jones (1976 – 2017) and SOCICO INC. Mr Jones agrees to take on a 100-year duty as the avatar of *SUFFERING MISUNDERSTOOD ARTIST*, with all the traits and duties described in the cultural consciousness of Mr Jones's era. The assignment is followed by a 100-year reward. Mr Jones can choose between the following:

Avatar *THE LAVISH LIFESTYLE OF A PUBLISHED AUTHOR*
Avatar *BLISS*

Avatar *EVERYTHING WILL BE GREAT IF I WIN THE LOTTERY*
Death

"Surely, this can't be legal," I say, but they both just shrug.

"You've got to read the fine print," he says again.

"But what am I meant to do?" I say. But I know the answer. "Oh," I say.

"Pretty cool, huh?" says the girl. "It just comes to you like that. That's how you get what you want here, too. Just... pick it out of the air."

The glass of whiskey in my hand is perfect. Deep, dark, smells like smoke and oak and barrel wood.

"There, you get it!" she says. "Listen, there will be new people arriving, I think a few of the ideas about war are due for updates today. But have a look around, okay? There are gods and concepts in the next room; most of the ideas are here. Anything you want can be drawn out of the air, and your room will be exactly like you expect it, so again... think smart." She smiles. Laughs. Heads back out into the reception area. Hikes her shorts. Spits. She's wearing overalls now.

Day 2.

I'm lonely. No one understands me here. No one ever understood me. Everyone thinks they can write. They don't understand the deep and discomforting process that goes into every word you bleed onto the page. I sip my whiskey, then get another, and drink until I pass out across my pages. I've not talked to any of the other avatars, yet. They wouldn't understand.

When I wake up, I've written a single word. 'The.' It's a good word, the definite article. It's strong and dependable. You can rarely go wrong with it. But now it feels all wrong on the page, so I cross it out and start over. If I have 100 years here, at least I can write my masterpiece.

Day 5.

The shadows that fell across the hardwood floors spoke volumes of the passing time. I see it. I do. I get that it's pompous, grand. Too many words to say nothing at all. But I've got time; I can get this right.

I stand up and walk to the gods' room. Thor and Zeus have been playing canasta against Buddha and a Japanese house god for a decade, according to Miss *Time Heals All Wounds*. She's the only pleasant company I've found in this goddamn hotel. Thor and Zeus are almost indistinguishable, and sometimes they swap their headgear to confuse people. Lightning strikes when they lose.

"How are they doing?" I whisper to Thaw – that's how they do it here, abbreviate your name to make it easier. "What's happening with the cards? They look all... brown."

She smiles. "Hello Smart," she whispers back. "They had to swap them with Mister *Never Trust Someone Who Won't Spit And Shake* over there, and they're really old." We watch them play for a little while. The Japanese house god always smiles, and it unnerves me. One would think that as the concept of a god, he'd understand that there is quite literally nothing to smile about.

"How's your novel going?" Thaw whispers. She touches my shoulder and I feel like there might – just might – be hope for a happy ending, after all. When the novel's done. When I've gotten the recognition I deserve.

"It's fighting me," I say. "I've got this scene in my head, but I can't get it out on the paper. Words feel poor, meaningless, cardboard gestures – they don't measure up to the castle of refinement I have in my mind..." and then I talk about myself until her eyes glass over, and I get angry, break my whiskey glass and accuse of her not understanding. No one even takes notice. This is who they expect me to be.

Day 83.

The shadows spoke volumes. In them, the passing time was held in place, caged in hardwood floor. The hairs on her dark skin rose to greet the winds, but still I didn't close the window. My heart was in the shadows, not in her physical form. I like it. The opening has the right tone to it, and I can imagine her there, sprawled out on the bed next to me – next to *him* – as he watches the shadows cross the floor. Her goosebumps are painted on the canvas of my mind. A close-up, perhaps of the nape of her neck, or maybe it's the soft skin along her side. In my mind, I follow them down, see the wind passing across her naked body, the small of her back, her bum, her thighs, and I'm aroused and angry. This is not what I've written. The delicate tenderness in her sleeping face, the soft gust of wind, how it enters through the window – from which you can hear crickets and an owl, perhaps two people laughing on their way home from the bar – none of that is in my words. They simply will not do. I drink.

Day 125.

"You're a moron, then!" I yell, and he stands up so fast my glass topples and 40-year-old scotch trickles down onto the carpet. "Now look what you've done!"

"Excuse me," he growls, "but if you think you can simply make a claim like that for us to accept it, without challenge, without... without... Ach! Reasoning with you is like pissing your pants to stay warm. Initially quite exciting, but ultimately a fool's folly."

"You're a walking cliché!" I shout. He slams his fists on the table, spilling my new glass of whiskey and startling Thaw, who's been watching us with an amused expression.

"We all fucking are!" he shouts. "That's why we're here in the first place!" He storms off, and I throw another glass after him, just for good measure.

"He's an imbecile," I say. "An amoeba. He's something you find in deep dark oceans, stuck to other organisms, barely even a leech. How *dare* he."

Thaw places my face in her hands and kisses my forehead. "He's *Mister There Are No More Original Ideas*," she says, smiling. "What did you expect him to say?"

I yell and throw my pages into the fire. The paper crumples, the edges burn, and then the whole stack combusts. She sighs.

"Again, Smart? You're going to burn all of it again?"

"He's right. It's rubbish! Absolute derivative drivel." Then I sob into her lap until she goes to bed.

Day 714.

As she sleeps, I watch the shadows. They creep across the hardwood floor, slowly, as if not to spook me. Their quiet passing speaks volumes about time. Their dark bars keep us in cages. Her dark skin... It's okay, but it's not the same. I haven't been able to even approach her skin for a good month now. Thaw sits across from me, looks up at me over the top of her book now and then, smiles and stretches like a cat. She's so naive. How she survived in the real world, I'll never know. When I first saw her naked, after a few months here – *or was it days?* – I spent ages tracing the broad scars across her back. They made ridges and valleys, mountains and trenches. Her back was a landscape of deep trauma and slow healing.

"What happened to you?" I said, and she rolled over onto her back, half-closed eyes and a slow smile.

"We liked to keep things in the family. Secrets, angers, bloodlines..." She spoke slowly, with long, lingering pauses. Took the time to pick and polish each word in her story. Made them beautiful and delicious. Moments later, I realised I wasn't paying attention. I was too busy describing her way of speaking in my head.

Her scarred back has replaced the goosebumped skin of my opening. It has blinded my inner eye and blocked my understanding of my own story. Whenever she smiles at me over the top of her book, I feel like punching her in the face. *Idea thief*, I think. *You've stolen all my thoughts*. Then she stretches like a cat again, and all I want is to wrap her up and kiss her in the garden.

Day 716.
"I'm Mister *Suffering Misunderstood Artist*!" I scream. "Why did you even *think* I'd be faithful to you? Sleeping around is what I'm here for! That's how I learn! How I ache! How I find my muses!"

She doesn't cry. She just picks her stuff out of my bedside table and steps across the broken glass on my carpet. Her feet bleed into the long fibres, mixing with whiskey, cigarette ash and glass.

"Bye, Smart," she says and goes back to her own room. I don't know which one it is. There are too many options to start knocking on doors. I trash the room and light it on fire. The night porter sighs and invents me a new one.

Day 16,500.
Only 20,000 more days to go. In 20,000 days, my masterpiece must be done, and they won't stop harassing me. Every few months, a new university class, or ten, starts studying me as an idea, a concept, a goal. I'm sent to the Gold Room, where their words whip and cuddle me for a few weeks while I try – really try – to work. But who can work surrounded by such luxury? Or admiration? Or spite? And then, when I get back down here, to the restaurant, I miss my luxurious surroundings and wish I'd taken better advantage of them.

The whiskey is better there too. But too distracting, when you come right down to it. Thaw is dating Miss *The Worst That Can Happen Just Ain't That Bad*, and their naive optimism infuriates me.

Day 21,411.

The infinite park is so fake it makes my teeth hurt. I walk and walk, through saccharine sweet wildflower meadows and impeccably carved hilltops. Everything is drawn to be so beautiful, so pristine. I disagree with Mister *Capitalism Is The Only System That Works* and Mister *Womansplaining Is The Real Problem* (he's new) – there's no beauty in this artificial construct. They love it. "Why have natural when you can have perfect?" they say, and it makes me question their right to exist. Clearly, they don't understand life. Love. Lust.

There has to be an edge. I walk and walk, run when I can. We never get tired here. Not really. So I keep marching on, knowing that the day won't end until I decide to go to sleep. Hundreds of hours have passed. Still no edge. In four days, Thaw is retiring. She's been the avatar of *Time Heals All Wounds* for 100 years, and someone new – someone different – is going to take over. I asked Thaw which reward she'd choose. She wouldn't even tell me her options.

Something's different with the next hill. Near the bottom, strong winds have pushed a tree over. But it's not covered in beautiful moss or climbing vines; it's not the perch for a curious hare, watching me with its glassy eyes as it chews on endless clovers. This tree is just dead. The path leading up the hill doesn't look enticing. It's not covered in hard tracks, easy to walk and satisfying to climb. Even before I step onto it, I know it's uneven, crooked, hard to walk and wet in places. It takes me longer to get up this one stretch than I've spent on the last three miles. I get out of breath. My heart races. I sweat and drip and cough up roughly 21,000 days' worth of cigarette smoke. And then I'm there.

The edge. It's nothing. It's a big black chunk of nothing. Outside the grounds of SOCICON INC, nothing stretches out like a starless night. No, not starless. There are flashes out there. Glimpses and flashes of ideas. Small pops and bursts of colour as things happen outside the social consciousness below. But then they melt and merge into the dark, and the grounds feed on the idea. SOCICON is everything. There's nowhere to go.

That's what I write. I conjure up paper. Pens. I write until my fingers bleed, my wrists hurt, my arms swell and darken. This is my masterpiece. The work I've been waiting for. 20,000 words. 50,000 words. 80,000 words, written in front of the void. Staring into the abyss. Knowing it is in me.

Day 21,413.

"I don't get it," she says. "It's just... I'm sure it's very good, I just don't get it." She smiles. Shrugs. Keeps packing. Stacks her belongings into suitcases, boxes. They'll bring them to her new room. She's taken on a new avatar, but won't tell me which one.

I've been reading for hours. It's good. Really good. I've written her scars with beautiful precision. I've made them immortal. Symbols of the beauty of humanity's flawed consciousness. Our ideas being wounds on the surface. The scars they create being beautiful. A landscape of ideas and concepts, gods and heroes, politics and truths. She doesn't get it.

"What do you mean you don't get it? It's obvious!" I say. For once, I don't want whiskey.

"It's very beautiful, all that about scars and the car accident and how that lady was like... evil or something? It's good. I... I just don't understand what it's about. I've never been good at literature stuff. Ask one of the professors? Ask Mister *The Pen Is Mightier Than The Sword*?"

They don't get it.

Day 21,416.

She comes back as Miss *Honesty Is The Best Policy*, choosing the avatar that lets her do something new. Something she's never done. And now she's angry. Each word she says lashes through my flesh and makes me flinch. I'm cowering under the accusations. About me, my book, my writing, my persona.

"I was there for you every day," she says, "I supported you, encouraged you. We've had nearly 60 years together here, and not *once*, not a SINGLE TIME, have you thanked me." And it goes on from there. I don't care about that. I know I'm difficult. But she calls my book "pompous word-masturbation", and I scream and call her too stupid to understand. The fight goes on.

Day 21,421.

"I'm Mister *Suffering Misunderstood Artist*," I sob,

"How did you expect me to behave?"

I read my book. It is good.

Day 28,000.

Only 8,500 more days. Honesty says I drink too much. That I have a problem. That my inflated sense of self is getting in the way of forming meaningful relationships. I point out that I've been playing canasta every other day for 26 years, and that I always play with the same people: Mister *Mansplaining*, Miss *Art Knows no Boundaries* and Mister *True Artists Are Rarely Appreciated In Their Lifetime*. She says I'm proving her point, not mine.

I read my book. It is good.

Day 36,493.

"What do you want to do with our last week in this constellation?" I ask. We're tangled up in a deep knot. A total of 100 years of arguments, fights, lovemaking, passion and pain lie strewn across our bed, upon our skin, across our faces and sticking to our hair.

"What do you mean, 'in this constellation'?" She smiles and stretches in that way that drives me crazy. The way I haven't fully been able to describe. The endless challenge between me and paper.

"Well, I'll be back as another avatar," I say. "We'll be able to do things slightly differently then."

She chews on her lip, stares into the ceiling. "I don't think I want us to continue if you come back," she says. "It's been nice, but exhausting. I think I want to try something else."

"But I'll come back as someone happier," I say, "someone less tortured. I can choose between *Bliss*, *Everything Will Be Great If I Only Win The Lottery*, and *The Lavish Lifestyle Of A Published Author*. Don't you want to try dating *Bliss*?" I say, and kiss her stomach as if to prove my point.

"I just don't think I'll like you as much," she says. "This is over."

Day 36,499.

I refuse a farewell party, and I don't even go around to say goodbye to everyone. It's been strange, saying goodbye to people who disappear one day then show up with a whole new outlook on life the next. I won't be that person. My masterpiece is still good. Honesty still won't get back together, and I'm a few points down in our canasta tournament. Better to just rice out the day.

"Mister *Suffering Misunderstood Artist* to reception," says the pleasant voice on the calling system. It's earlier than I expected, but I've waited long enough. I grab my masterpiece and shake the other players' hands.

"Bye for now," I say, and they nod. Some African god takes over my hand and joins the game. He plays more aggressively than me. I bet he'll be back up on points soon.

A woman waits for me in reception. I recognise her as the woman who was Miss *Angel Of Mercy* when I first arrived. There really was something wrong with her back then. Rumour said she'd needed a full reprogramming as there wasn't a single consistent myth about angels of mercy in the social consciousness to keep her going. It had been brutal.

She looks me up and down, sees my masterpiece and nods.

"This way," she says. "Your masterpiece, I assume?"

"Yeah," I say.

"Been a while since we had an author. The *Suffering Misunderstood Artist* avatar has predominantly been painters lately, but an author. Good. Good for you."

"How many of me have there been?" I say. Her head wrinkles. They always get confused when you ask them to place something in time.

"Maybe... 6,000?"

"But–" I protest, but her face flickers before I can get another word out.

"In total," she says, "there will be 6,000. You are number... less than 6,000. I don't know. Yes! I don't know. Yes! I don't know."

She walks down a long corridor I've often seen but never bothered with. Right at the end, there's a door marked 'Library'.

"There's a library here?" My face drops so fast I feel like I'll faint. "There's been a library here all along, and no one ever told me?"

"Oh, no one ever goes to the library," she says. Shrugging. It's beautiful. Huge. Hundreds and hundreds of titles. Not huge, but beautiful.

"Here we are," she says.

"What?"

"The space for your book." She points to an empty slot on the shelf between two other thick bound volumes from *Suffering Misunderstood Artist George Billinghurst* and *Suffering Misunderstood Artist Jaqueline DaZazabar.*

"I don't understand," I say.

"This is where you put them at the end of your term. This is the room of masterpieces by suffering misunderstood artists. Like you."

I look around again. There are paintings, records, sculptures, odd clothes, dresses, jewellery. As I watch, the room stretches out in every direction. Thousands upon thousands of pieces that simply aren't that good.

"But no one ever comes here," I say. "You just told me no one ever comes to the library."

"Nah," she says. "The avatars are mostly too preoccupied with their own theorems."

I walk slowly, touch what I can, pick up books and read a few pages here and there. *Mine is better*, I think. *Mine is better.*

"Isn't there... anywhere else we could put it? Can't it be on the shelves in the restaurant?"

She smiles. "Sorry, hon. This is where your book belongs. No one would understand it anyway."

I swallow.

"You should see the other library though," she says, "The one filled by the avatars of *The Joy Of Creation Is Reward Enough Itself* – so bright and weird. No one ever goes there either. But... you know. That's kind of the point."

"I see," I say, and place my masterpiece on the shelf. I run my finger over its spine. "Hey... would you read it?" I say. "It's very good."

She looks at me. There's some definite pity crossing her face, and it would have pissed me off if I wasn't so empty.

"Maybe," she says. "I'm very close with Miss *Never Say Never.*" And then she laughs and walks toward the door.

Day 36,500.
I choose death.

Those Who Grow up
in Summer

"What do you think it is?" said little Billy the Bubble. They all had the same question, but because he'd asked it first, they all pretended like it wasn't something they needed an answer to – not yet.

"Shut up, Billy," said Molly, who didn't have a nickname, because she had two older brothers and a very solid right fist. "We can't just *know* things like that. We have to study it closely, make notes and observe first."

She shook out the contents of her pockets: a bit of a broken ruler, some string, half a magnifying glass and a graphite stub. She thrust the stub at Nicholas the Nerd, because he was the only one who knew how to handwrite.

"You take this down," she said. She held the piece of ruler next to the little thing and furrowed her brow for several seconds before stating, "It's about as high as my left pointing finger."

"That's not how you do it," said the Nerd. "You're supposed to find out how many inches it is."

Molly rolled her eyes. "*Obviously*," she said. "But you can't do that with a broken ruler, can you? I only have inches 16 to 20, and it ain't that long, is it?"

The Nerd wasn't quite as scared of Molly as the other kids were, but even he knew to fear her 'Obviously'. You just didn't call her out like that. Not because she'd punch you – although she might – but because being one of the people Molly played with was a much better deal than being one of the kids who only heard about it later.

Molly knew how to make things happen. She wasn't afraid of adults, and she knew how to start adventures. The only reason they'd found this thing was because Molly considered a 'DO NOT ENTER' sign an advertisement.

"I think," she had told the Nerd once, "that the grown-ups put those up because they want to keep those bits to themselves. They're jealous, you see, 'cause we get to have fun all the time, while they just have to, you know, go to work and stuff. So they try and save some places for later, but they'll probably be dead by the time they get to visit them again. So they won't mind if we go in, not really. 'Cause they'll never find out."

Nicholas had never doubted the flawless logic of Molly's explanation – not even the time Billy the Bubble almost drowned in the bomb crater. Adults, he figured, would have been able to swim in the crater no problem, so they must have been saving the pond for a swim later. Although, when it came right down to it: with such long legs, it would have been much harder for them to avoid the undetonated bomb at the bottom. Better, then, to let the kids swim there.

Molly looked like she was thinking about something. She screwed her eyes up and looked to the sky. "Here's a test, okay?" she said, turning to Nosebleed Nelly, who was chewing on her right plait and fiddling with the other.

"Okay," she mumbled.

"What is that colour called?"

"The lost colour," said Nosebleed.

Molly sighed exaggeratedly. "No... I mean what was its real name, before it was lost?"

Nosebleed shrugged. "Don't remember."

"Oh, I know, I know, I know!" said Bubble. One of his snotbubbles pulsated with each eager breath.

"Fine," said Molly, "what is it then?"

"Green," said Bubble.

"Oh yeah!" said Molly. "I mean, yes, that's right. Write down that it's green," she said to the Nerd. Then she leaned down close, until her nose practically touched it, and drew a long, deep, slow breath. "It smells... kind of like... nothing. It smells like nothing. At least nothing that I've smelled before."

"Can I try?" said Bubble.

She scoffed. "You keep your bubbles far away from this thing. Nerd, you try."

This was a rare act of favour, being entrusted with something other than recording Molly's own thoughts and movements. He got down on his knees, approached the frail little mystery and smelled it as if he was afraid it would break.

"Oh," he said. "It smells like my great-grandma – or at least, my mum has this bottle, and when you take the cap off, it smells real nice, and my mum says that's what my great-grandma used to smell like. Real nice like that."

Molly frowned. "I don't think we can say it smells like your great-grandma," she said. "Is it not called anything?

"'Fume', I think," the Nerd said, and shrugged.

"All right, write that then. What else… what else…?" She reached a finger out and poked it. "Oh!" she said as it bent to her touch. "It's all soft."

They all startled when they saw it move like that. They'd expected it to be hard and rigid – some sort of metal, maybe.

"What do you think it is?" said Molly, pretending Bubble hadn't asked the question to begin with.

"Is it a piece of clothing, maybe?" said Nosebleed.

"Doubt it," said Molly. "Where would the rest of it be? And why isn't it all… torn?"

"Maybe it's some sort of weapon," said Bubble. "Some sort of secret government spy weapon that finds smells in your brain so you say that it smells like that, even if it actually smells like poison because it's trying to kill you."

"Next!" said Molly.

"I think," said the Nerd, "and I don't *know*, okay? But I think, maybe, it could be… and don't laugh – but maybe it is a plant."

The others stared at him. The Nerd wasn't the one who usually made up fairy-tales. They had expected him to say it was a piece of rubber or some other ancient material; that's what he usually said when they found something interesting.

"Are you being serious? For serious?" said Molly. She looked at the same time excited and cross, as if trying to anticipate both treasure and treachery.

The Nerd bit his lip. "I know it sounds crazy," he

said. "But look at it. Comes out of the ground – check. Is green – check. Smells nice – check. Doesn't look like anything we have ever seen before – check. Kind of looks like something that hasn't existed for a hundred years – check. It certainly is a possibility," he said. "If anything we've ever found is a plant, this is it."

They all bent forward. None of them really knew what to say. For years, they had pretended to find plants. Imagined what green would look like when it was alive, not just ink on paper. Their whole lives, they had heard about the time before the bombs, how the Earth had been covered in the lost colour, and filled with foods that had colours and more than eight different flavours. Back when there was electricity, fuel and other types of magic they didn't fully understand. And now, they might have found it. A piece of this world of Before.

"What should we do?" said Molly, uncharacteristically pragmatic. This was important. "We should probably tell someone, right?"

They looked at each other. They all remembered what had happened when rumour had spread of a plant found over at the F18 camp. All the residents had been moved out of the camp and scattered around the different habitats. The whole place had been domed for weeks, and by the time the government left, it had all been picked apart in the search for a plant that wasn't even there.

"Maybe..." said Nerd. "But then again... if it is a plant, it will keep growing, get bigger and that. Maybe we should wait a few days. Just to, you know, make sure."

Molly dug around in the front pocket of her overalls until she found a thick needle. "You know what this means," she said, and they all did. Some occasions automatically call for a blood pact.

There was a rumour flying around F38 that summer. Rumours often flew around F38, but they were usually amongst the adults, and about someone hiding away an extra ration pack, or a settler having a connection in the Smoke. But this rumour was different. It belonged to the others – those who only got to hear about Molly's games after the fact. They whispered that Molly had found religion, suffered a brain injury or been given a beating by some older kids from F39. That whatever it was had left her meek and withdrawn, hiding around on mountaintops.

The rumour made sense. At least, Molly and her usual gang were rarely seen causing havoc any more. There were no sudden announcements that there would be a play in the container yard and that anyone who didn't come to watch them perform was rotten protein. Not a single time did angry parents march over to Molly's tent, and not once did Molly's father have to use his credits to pay for breakages or medicars.

In reality, of course, Molly and her gang were busy with their incredibly scientific experiment. They built a fort of old debris not far from the crater, where they could rest in the shadow as they watched the plant grow. They watched its leaves spread across the ground, and invented new words for its shades of green. They watched as its yellow head bloomed and drank its sweet smell in big deep gulps. They worried the smell was limited, that it would only last a certain number of sniffs, so they took turns smelling it, one at a time, wondering who would get the last sniff. Relieved that there always seemed to be one more.

"Do you think it's time we tell someone?" said the Nerd one day, making the others shuffle uneasily. They knew they'd let it go on for too long. That it was *definitely* a plant, and that this was no longer a small secret. Now, they were keeping a big secret. An *our parents could go to the box* kind of secret. But there was something else as well. If they told someone now…

"No," said Molly. "We're not telling anyone."

"But…" said the Nerd.

"Blood pact," said Molly, and the shuffling relaxed. They had made a blood pact, and they couldn't tell if they didn't all agree to. Molly didn't agree, so really, it was mostly her fault, if it came right down to it. They were just keeping the pact.

"Besides," said Molly, "I want to see how it ends."

They tried drawing its various stages, tried to capture the soft strands of the flower head and the thick texture of the leaves. Nosebleed was the best at drawing, but Bubble was quite good at getting the little details right. Molly managed to nick another four graphite stubs and some firebook pages from the school container. They bleached the pages in the sun, watched as the discarded words slowly disappeared off the kindling and made the pages pale enough to draw on. They hung the drawings on the walls of their fort, and Molly scrutinised each line and told them how to do better. Nosebleed was glad to have a proper job for once – she was always the lookout – and Bubble loved the opportunity to show that he could be clever like Nicholas the Nerd. Maybe not *as* smart, if you were picking very hard at it, but he was clever when it came to seeing things, and seeing things is important too. The Nerd wrote observations next to the drawings, measured the plant's increasing height in lengths of string, counted petals, leaves, even veins. This plant, the most beautiful thing they had ever seen, was so thoroughly documented that they had nothing to argue about.

"But that was a week ago," Molly might say as they discussed how long it had been since the flower was still tight in the middle. But all they had to do was look to the drawings, and they would show that there was still a tight centre just four days ago, and Molly would move on. The drawings hung side by side on the fort walls until the day Freddy the Fiddle came a little too close.

"What are you all doing?" he called from behind the fence.

"None of your business, Fiddle boy," shouted Molly, "and if you don't go away right now, I'll clock your teeth in!"

Fiddle wasn't very brave, so they didn't think he'd come back. But just in case, they made the flower a woven basket to hide it when they weren't there, and buried the drawings in the cold, scorched earth.

"I think the plant is dying," Bubble said one morning. They'd all been thinking it, but hoped someone else would say it first.

They tried to save it. Each of them smuggled bits of their water rations up to the fort, and crumbled protein rations onto the ground around it.

"Come on," Molly whispered, lying on her stomach right in front of the plant. "Stay, just a little longer." But a few days later, the yellow began fading, and soon a ghostly head sprung out.

"Guys," Molly said solemnly, holding her needle up. "We can never, ever tell anyone that we let the plant die…"

The others agreed, staring sadly at the whisper-thin, fuzzy head.

"Maybe we should give someone our drawings…" the Nerd suggested.

"Never! Tell! Anyone!" Molly said, underlining each word in the air with the needle. "Do we have to murder you, Nicholas the Nerd? Can we trust you or do we have to murder you?"

"You can trust me," he said, kicking at the dust.

"Guys!" said Nosebleed. "Look!"

A gust of wind picked up the plant's soft white tussles and carried the tiny spears through the air, Nicholas the Nerd felt Molly fumble at his side until she found his hand. He squeezed hers lightly. The four of them watched the last traces of flower tumble and dance away. None of them cried, not really.

About Time

I have 6,316 minutes left. I know this with an all-encompassing certainty that makes me unable to take advantage of a single one of them. Really, I just want to die.

When a baby is born, the doctor will say, "Congratulations, it's a girl!" or whatever your child is, quickly followed by, "Do you want the display?" The parents will cry, hug each other and the baby, and most of them will say, "Yes, of course! Of course, Doctor." And then they will wait anxiously, and hope that the baby's time doesn't run out while the display is being connected. Sometimes it does, of course. They give you your money back, then.

Even the very poorest of parents will try.

"Yes, Doctor, we want the display, but we can't afford it. Please, is there any other way?" The doctor will take two years from you both, because doctors are people too, and then she will give the child its display, but you don't get your time back if something happens.

My auntie turned up at our house four or five years ago. My mother was at first very happy; we hadn't heard from her in over a year. But as they spoke through the night, she became sad and angry – I had never seen Mami angry before – and she raged at my father and said "– to do SOMETHING –" and "– just not RIGHT! HOW CAN THEY–" and other fragments of anger that seeped up the stairwell. There, they landed on the five of us, perched on the top step. We didn't understand, of course, not at first, but the more we listened, the sadder we became.

My auntie had given birth to a secret baby. Secret, because the father was on the council, and no one on the council ever had children, and neither did he, of course. But he held her hand in the hospital and patted her forehead with a cold cloth. He fed her grapes, and flavour drink through a long straw, and whispered that she was doing great.

"Congratulations," the doctor said – my auntie said she was a beautiful doctor, but she'd looked sad, all the time – "It's a girl!"

My auntie and the father hugged each other and the baby, crying with happiness over this little perfect human.

"Do you want the display?" said the doctor. My auntie nodded and started handing the baby back, but the father grabbed her and said darkly, "Can you afford it?"

My auntie cried, screamed, begged the father to help pay. And he cried and explained, again and again, that his money was tracked, and so were his minutes. He could not pay for a child. He would lose everything. The doctor left them alone for an hour, my auntie begged and cried, the councillor begged and cried, but he wouldn't change his mind.

"Spend the time you have with the baby." he kept saying. Placing the tot in her arms, again and again. He tried to make her focus on the baby's smooth skin, her tiny fingernails and soft, feathery hair.

"Feed her," he said, but my auntie refused. The display has to be attached before the first feeding.

"Feed her, you don't want to miss that feeling," he said, but she didn't listen. She didn't listen to any of his explanations or excuses.

"People survived for thousands of years without the display. She'll be fine. It's exciting not knowing... in a way..." He hid his face in expressions.

My auntie called for the doctor and asked how many minutes she would need.

"Two years," said the doctor. She was kind, this doctor. You can't transfer more than two years in a day.

My auntie, like all the women in my family, will become very old, and so she gladly cut a few years of her own life to know the details of her daughter's. But when the doctor came back, it was running, panting.

"Three minutes," she gasped, near tossing the baby into my auntie's arms. "She only has three more minutes." She stared at the father. "Did you know?" she said, but the father waved her out of the room and closed the door behind her.

It is this that haunts my auntie. The implication that the father knew.

They say your minutes are determined at random, a great big cosmic lottery. And although that is probably true, for the most part, everyone suspects there are people who know the numbers. My auntie couldn't transfer any more minutes. The father refused to. The doctor could not. My auntie lost her baby without ever feeding her, and now she lives in our attic and sings about birds in the morning.

I keep checking my display as the minutes tick down. A little more than four days. I walk through the city, try to smell and touch everything, but I mostly just check my display.

I will miss my auntie's singing. I will miss lots of things. Except, of course, I won't. Because I will be dead, and the dead don't miss anything at all. That's what they teach us in school – that death is painless and empty. It is natural, quick; it's fine.

When I was born, the doctor only said congratulations, and then he hesitated for a long while.

"Is it a boy?" said my father, who loved all three of his daughters but really wanted a son.

"It is a girl?" said my mother, who knew the women in her family always bear women.

"No," said the doctor. "Do you want the display?" My parents cried and hugged each other, and they didn't see me again for hours. I was a beautiful baby, said my mother. A very beautiful baby, with lots of hair and big eyes.

"A little like a lizard, but not too much," she told me once, when she had drunk a couple of glasses of wine, danced with my father on the kitchen floor and talked about the five of us as if we weren't there.

"You were such a beautiful baby," she smiled, "but they told us, 'She is not a girl, he is not a boy, but he's probably one or the other. You just have to wait and see.'"

My father laughed. "But they were wrong," he said. "You aren't one or the other, but a little bit of both. But that's okay," he said, nodding, "it's okay."

The five of us mouthed the next part with them. They never noticed, but we did, and it made us feel like we belonged together, the five of us and them.

"You are all strange," my mother started.

"...in your own ways," my father said.

"But we love you," they said together. Then they'd linger, exchange glances, then blurt out, "Because it's too late to hand you back!" Then they'd lean on each other and gasp for breath, as if they hadn't said this a hundred times before. As if the sentence made sense; as if it was actually funny outside the bubble of the two of them. We loved them for their delusion. The five of us rolled our eyes and shook our heads, but kindly. And we danced with them on the kitchen floor, my sisters and I.

I think my father was proud of me for being not one or the other, but a little bit of both. He'd always wanted a son, and in the absence of a son, the second best thing was a void in which all gender expression disappeared. They named me Tomodachi – a word for 'friend' in one of the ancient languages – and called me Chi, because it was easier.

I left them last night. I kissed my mother goodbye, and she cried.

"Let me give you some years," she said. "Let me give you two, your father will give you two, we have many left. Please," she begged. And I kissed her again, and led her into the arms of my father.

"I wish I could give you some years..." said my youngest sister, Morvarid. She was also crying, and didn't want to meet my eyes. I held her to me, kissed her hair, and whispered that I was happy to have had her for a sister. I had given her more years than I cared to remember. I had fed her minutes to keep her alive. She did not want to seem ungrateful. But I know, if she wasn't still too young, she would have given me all the time she could. My little sister is as tired as I am.

My other sisters didn't offer. They had offered me a few years each the night before. But they, like me, had given their years to Morvarid, and didn't have many more to offer. When I had turned them down a couple of times, they stopped asking. They treasured their years, like jewels. They hugged me closely and stuck little treats into my pockets the way they always had, and the way I was sure they would keep doing for Morvarid as long as she could find more years.

My father reached out his hand and held mine for a long time.

"I love you," he said. I nodded, grabbed my backpack and left them all behind with the rest of my things. I left them with their minutes, and their hours and their days, because really. I just want to die.

My auntie waited in the driveway; she had promised to drive me to the next city. We sailed in the first layer, the slow lane. It was close enough to the ground that I could see people on the street, wasting their minutes. My auntie cried all the way there, but we didn't speak. Instead, I sang one of the songs I've heard her sing in the evenings, and after a while, she joined in. Our voices were light and shone through the car and the city, across the fields and through the mountains. When we got there, she offered me a year or two, but I turned it down politely.

"Give them to Morvarid," I said, "if it's needed." She nodded. She stuck some treats in my pocket, and I bowed deeply, the way you do for your elderly aunts. As she sailed away I tried to keep singing, but I could no longer remember the tune.

Morvarid is defective. Some children are. She was born with 54,771,194 minutes: impressive, even for women in my family.

"Mami," said Zawadi, my oldest sister, "the baby's minutes are faster than mine." The baby was about six months old then, already being a little person with faces and sounds. For weeks after, I can only remember my parents running. Running to the doctor, running in corridors, running to the shop, running to the baby, all the time running. The baby's minutes disappeared too fast. They drained away between my mother's fingers, and there was nothing the doctors could do. But they stayed in the hospital for weeks to make sure.

Zawadi, Meimei – my second oldest sister – and Ajabu – who is four years older than me – took turns making dinner and taking care of me. When we had eaten, they would make me wear one of the ancient masks off the wall, and I would chase them around the house. They would hide, and I would seek. They would try to steal a flag, and I would guard it. We played and played and played, while we waited, and I remember them as wonderful days.

When my parents came home with the baby, I went running at them, wearing the scariest mask off the wall.

"Mami! Dobi!" I cried, because I had missed them so. The baby saw me and screamed, like they do.

"Chi!" my mother shouted. "Don't startle the baby! Her minutes go too fast."

I tore my mask off, and kissed the baby on her soft head. "I'm sorry," I said, "I'm sorry, baby. In four years, I can give you some of mine."

When she turned two and was ready to receive her name, my parents named her Morvarid. My mother is an expert on the ancient languages, and she had searched until she found a name that fit. Morvarid meant pearl, and she was a pearl. There was a grain of her – a good heart, a beautiful smile, a decent head – and around it we wrapped layer after layer of minutes. She ran through them at varying speeds. A whole year could disappear in a day; another might last a week or two. But we refilled of our own minutes, and the more she got, the slower they disappeared. It was as if something in her very blood made minutes flow, drip and rush through her veins. It affected those around her too. We soon realised that the mechanism that kept us from transferring more than two years at a time didn't kick in when we transferred to Morvarid. She was insatiable. She could dry you out if you didn't pay attention.

She's one of my favourite humans. I have given her more than 60 years of my time, and I don't regret a single one. She lives under the weight of all our years and it has made her beautiful, inside and out, but it will not make her old.

We made the decision when she was eight, because a decision had to be made.

"We will do what we can to keep her alive until she's 16," my father said at the end of the talk. His face had aged. The discussion of all the time that would disappear had carved lines into his face. "When she's 16, she can start trading, and... she can decide for herself."

Trading. She could start trading. There aren't many things a 16-year-old with such an appetite for years could trade, not many things that would pay enough. But she was turning into a beautiful girl... We didn't want to think about that.

My parents have bought her many years. We sold the big house, and most of the masks off the wall. We sold the ancient books, and my mother stopped working as a teacher – a job she loved – and started working as an advisor for a private relic collector. She hated the job, but the money was good, and she took her payment in years whenever she could.

But Morvarid's years have been running faster and faster. Now it takes more than nine of our years to give her one. We have kept almost running out of her years, and we've bled our family dry. My auntie will no longer be a very old woman. My mother will no longer be a very old woman. My father has little more than ten years left. And I...

I gave Morvarid my last 48 years two days ago. She screamed and cried, but I held her down. My parents came running and tried to pull me off her; my sisters came running and tried to lift me off. They were all too late.

"Mami," I said, and held my mother's face in my hands, feeling her soft skin under my fingers, "this should get her to 16, if not longer. I'm tired, and I want to die. Tomorrow, we will have a big dinner, and then I'm going to go." My auntie had come running, and stood with closed eyes in the stairs.

"What have you done?" said my father, weaving his big hands through his thin hair, grasping it as for support.

"Chi..." said Zawadi.

"Chi..." said Meimei. Ajabu said nothing, but bowed deeply. Meimei bowed. Zawadi bowed. My auntie bowed. My parents were clutching Morvarid and crying, but I think my father bowed too.

It's not that I don't like living. Living is fine. It's whatever. I've never been green numbered, so I've never had to do any work hours for the government. My family has been well enough off for me to do whatever I want. But I don't want to do anything. My days are all the same, and I find so few things fun. I don't care about girls, and I don't care about boys. I don't want a job, or a career. I find no pleasure in toxdrinks or art, ancient relics or technology. I have watched my display every day, feeling a slow desperation creep over me. There're still so many minutes. Still so many days. I have lived slowly. But Morvarid lives with her entire body. She loves everything, and she finds pleasure in the strangest places. How much better for her to burn through the years I'm wasting.

As I walk through the city, I don't regret a single thing. But I'm bored. Four days left.

I pass a young couple on a staircase. They're crying and clutching a baby.

"I have to go," she says.

"Please… Just one more minute," he says, pulling her back by her arm. I see a car waiting. Industrial. She's been blue numbered, a young mother – that's rare. Her display beeps. She has one minute left to get into the car. This is measured closely; the system is fair, but strict.

"Let me give you a Grade-A hour," I say to her. She stares at me.

"What?"

"Let me give you a Grade-A hour."

"Yes! Do it! Let hi– her?" says the young man.

"Are you sure? They're expensive…" she says, but I wave it away, connect my display and ask for a Grade-A hour for transference. It annoys me to see it only costs me 26 hours, but it's a start. She notices the low number left and grows pale.

"Don't worry," I smile, "it's okay." The car sails away. "Enjoy your hour."

They both hug me, and I don't pull away. Why not have a hug? Why not?

Colours tend to run in families, although they're supposed to be assigned by aptitude. I wonder how much genetics has to do with your aptitude for government work as opposed to mine work. At least no one has to work for more than two years at once, but two years is a long time when you have a baby. I wonder if the man will name the baby without her, and I wonder why only green and gold bands can buy Grade-A hours, when we're the ones who need them the least.

I have 4,409 minutes left. I walk past the aftermath of an accident. Two paramedics are lifting a limp body into their ambulance. I hear the closest one talking to someone through a communicator. He grabs the limp body's wrist and says, "42 minutes. On this one, that is. The driver has about 16,000 left, but he's got his cranium cracked open so he'll take a bit of work…" He closes the door, and they sail up to the third layer and zoom away. They can fix everything these days. Almost.

The doctors waited for me to decide, and show, if I was one or the other or a little bit of both. They had procedures, they told me. They could help me look on the outside how I felt on the inside. For years, I said, "I *do*," and eventually, they stopped asking. I threw make-up and pearls on, but the void devoured it. I threw boots and suits and ties and heels on, but the void chewed them all up. It just doesn't care, so I don't either. People call me, "Welcome to our store, M… mi… si… mam?" And I smile, and accept their titles, because they don't matter to me.

"My name is Chi," I say and shake their hand. "I'm neither." Eventually, they stop worrying so much and just call me, "Welcome to our store, how may we assist you?" and it works for all of us, I think.

No one knows me here. Occasionally, people turn, but not often. Most people, old people, know that it doesn't much matter. Young people, however, are curious. They want to know if they can want me or not. If it's okay, or if their bodies are betraying them. This city is less conservative than mine, despite being just a few hours drive away. Desperate people sell minutes on the streets here. 40 Ron for a minute. It's not cheap, but neither is tox, and I'm betting that's what they need the money for. I wonder if my parents ever bought time from one of these people. I hope they didn't. I don't like to think about Morvarid's layers being brittle, fuelled by hunger and longing.

An old man is going up to one of these hungry people – a woman with huge knots in her hair, and grey bruises up and down her arm. I walk closer, curious.

"It's just, I want to make it to my daughter in time, and it's so terribly hard to see..." the old man says. I don't think the woman can even see his face.

"D'ya w'nt t'buy a minute?" she slurs, moving her head back and forth in an attempt to get him in focus.

"Oh, no, I don't think so, I just can't see if I still have time..." he says, but she doesn't listen.

"40 Ron f'r'a minute," she continues, "2 Len f'r'n hour. 'S like ten minutes f'free".

"No, thank you very much, I just..."

She scoffs. "Wh't'ya wast'n m'time for then?" she yells, and the man steps back in horror.

"I beg your pardon, I –" but she's turned her back to him and is showing her little cardboard sign to other bystanders. I walk over to the old man.

"Hey," I say.

"Oh, hello young man," he says, and I don't correct him. I bow.

"May I be of any assistance?" I ask, and keep my head down until he has acknowledged me.

"Child," he says, and I lift my head. "Such good manners. Like the old times!"

"I have been well raised, grandpa," I say, and the honorary title makes him smile.

"Could you tell me how much time I have left?" he says, holding out his frail wrist to show me his display.

"A little less than four hours," I say. I swallow. I don't know why, but I like this old man.

"Oh," he says, and his face falls a thousand miles through the earth, and leaves a burning trail in the soil. "I was going... but I suppose..." He turns to walk away, but I put my arm around his shoulder.

"Please, grandpa," I say, "let me know how I can help."

"Oh, nothing, nothing," he says. "I was just hoping to take a bus to Nikoro to see my daughter before... she's just got a new baby, yesterday, and I..." Nikoro is only a few hours away, I know, but he would have to rush to even make it in time to say hello.

"Please, let me give you some time," I say, and start connecting my display. He shakes his head and steps back.

"No, I couldn't, I cannot steal time from the young, it would not be right..." I understand his distress. The old should not accept time from the young. It's just not how it's done.

"Dearest grandpa," I say, and bow again. "Please do not think of it as stealing from me. Let it be my present to your new grandchild. I would like to gift him or her a day with her grandpa, as it is a gift I wish someone had given me. I must insist," I say. He really is of the old school. He's tearing up.

"Thank you," he says and grabs my hand. "Thank you. Please give me the honour of your name so I can tell them who the gift is from."

"My name is Tomodachi," I say. His face shines.

"Tomodachi!" he says. "Friend! In the old language!" He laughs and kisses my hands. His face is rounder than the moon, and I let him kiss me. Why not? Why not let him kiss my hands? I don't tell him that it isn't *my* old language, because I don't know for certain it's not. My mother has spoken so much of old languages that I don't know which is ours and which we simply love. I give the man 24 hours. He will not accept more. He tries to give me some money, but I will not take it. I have 2,898 minutes left. He wishes me a long and fruitful life, and for our paths to cross again. I wish him the same.

I'm getting tired, and that pleases me. A few more hours and I can go to sleep. Sleeping is a great way of spending time. A good night will bite out two big chunks of time, chew them and swallow them before you even notice. Morvarid sleeps very little. That thought makes me homesick, and for a while, I play with the idea of calling home. Making sure everyone's all right. But, no, I think better of it. They've said their goodbyes and are waiting for the call to come and pick up my body. I remind myself to leave time to bathe.

Darkness falls slowly, and my feet have started to hurt. Night brings out other people, and I sit down and look at them all for a while. It strikes me that most people, yes, almost all people, are unconcerned with their minutes. As I sit there, hardly anyone checks their display at all. They laugh and chat as if time is endless and slow. A girl sits next to me for a while, chatting about how her friend is supposed to meet her here, but probably has met some man. Two boys walk up to me, drinks in hand, and ask if I'm male or female, if I want a beating, if I'm looking for trouble. But they get bored quickly, as they always do, and start walking after a group of girls.

There are still hundreds of cars sailing above us. Occasionally, an ambulance or police vessel zooms past, up in the third layer, and I can see their blinking lights like meteors in the night sky. I wonder if there are still places where you can see stars. Not just the big ones – on a clear night in the countryside, you can see the Big Dipper and the Belt of Orion, if the season is right and you have keen eyes. I mean places where you can see the thousands and thousands of stars they used to see. When there were constellations enough for the whole year, and some people still knew stories about them. I wonder if they were all as clear as the moon, and if they really twinkled. 2,511 minutes left. I fall asleep and wake up with the sun. 2,189 minutes left.

You can't kill yourself here, not really. You can speed up the time, run towards death with open arms, but the last 24 hours can't be given away. That's just the rule. You can spend the minutes as payment, sure, but you can't empty them into someone else's account or make them all go away. I once tried to jump from the top of the Negaimasu Tower. I don't know what I thought would happen, probably nothing at all. But I sang through the air like a bullet, stretched out my arms and felt the air against my face, and I laughed until I heard the crack of every bone in my body. They can fix everything these days. Almost.

They've made it so that you can use almost all the minutes of your last day as payment, but not the last 60. It's a safety mechanism, I suppose. A way to make sure you have enough time left to put your affairs in order and call your mother before you go. I have a day and a half left. A bit over 12 hours I can give away, freely, and then it's just about waiting. I'm hungry, but I don't see the point in buying anything. The city is still quiet and damp, the sun is still rubbing sleep out of her eyes and hasn't yet started lacing the city in gold. Everything is grey and soft, and I have become cold to my bones.

I pass a diner. Its bright yellow light flows out onto the pavement like molasses. My legs go slow and tired as I walk past its huge windows advertising authentic inspired flavours and bio-vegetables. Why not have a meal? Why not? It's warm inside, and except for two Timers in the corner, I'm the only customer. The Timers' tallies beep when I enter; they throw sidelong glances at them, shrug, and continue through their food. I sit at the counter.

"Hello doll," says the fat lady behind the bar. She's the largest person I have ever seen, and she's beautiful and unkempt like a huge oak in autumn. Her hair is piled on top her head, pushing against bobby pins and clips, wrestling loose in new places all the time. Her hands constantly move across the pile, catching strands and pushing pins further into her 'do. She grins, and I'm sure I could make my tongue disappear in her dimples.

"Y'hungry?" she says. "Y'look starved!"

I study the menu she slapped down in front of me. I don't recognise any of the names. It is a traditions' restaurant: it mimics the style and flavours of the past. I close the menu and shrug.

"If you could only eat one thing, and it would be the last thing you ever ate, what would you pick?" I say. I try to smile broadly to make her think it's a joke, but this woman is smart.

"Y'runnin' out of time, honey?" she says, and pats my hand. It is hidden completely under hers.

"Yes, but that's okay. This is how I wanted it." I say.

She tuts. "Y'need noodles. Mushroom. I'll make you something nice. Here," she says and pours me a huge glass of something pink and translucent. It has a faint glow, which makes me smile. I haven't had an isodrink for years. It's sweet and sticky. It fills my mouth with memories of being little. Of Zawadi and Meimei giving me sips of their iso under the table, even though my mother had expressly told them that no one under four could drink it. It tastes of Morvarid's first birthday. It tastes of thinking there would be something better in the world, if I just waited a day or two longer. I smile.

"Gets you up in the morn', dunnit?" she smiles. I don't know how old she is. She sounds old. She sounds like she should be wrinkly and frail, and smell vaguely of dust and camphor. But her cheeks are full and fleshy, and not a single wrinkle is visible in her face. I want to hug her.

"Used to feed it to the children all the time," she chatters on as she cooks behind the back counter. She waddles back and forth, here, there, chopping and panting and wiping sweat on the back of her arm. I can hear the pneumatics in her leg supports hiss and whirr as she moves. "No one told us the iso could be bad back in those days, y'know. Can get you right messed up." She chats on and on and I listen attentively, but can't hear a single word she says. Some died, some didn't. She eats to forget and remember, but it's okay, because she meets enough people who give her minutes and hours and days for her cooking, she says, so she can pay for all the medical expansion she will ever need.

"I see," I say, drinking.

What she puts in front of me is not on the menu. I know, because every single thing on the menu is served with some sort of bun or bio-chips. This is soup, or resembles soup. There is broth, yes, and noodles. There are small green bits of bio-veg, and something brown and soft and salty.

"Mushrooms," she nods. "Don't get them that much anymore. Seem to have gone right out of fashion because they never died off, li'l buggers. They're good for your soul though. Eat!" she says, plunging a spoon into my bowl. I eat. It's tasty. I don't recognise the flavours, and that surprises me. Not that I thought I had tasted everything, but I thought I had tasted enough. This is delicious. I wish I could drain away my last minutes here and now, so I would die with this taste still in my mouth. Mami would have loved this. I drink every last drop of the broth, and make sure I haven't left any pieces of mushroom along the rim.

"Thought that'd make your cheeks glow, doll," says the lady.

"You are beautiful," I say. I don't know why – it just tumbles out of my mouth.

"Oh, I know *that*, doll. But thank you though, mighty nice of you to compliment an old lady."

"How…" I pause. "How old are you, if you don't mind me asking?"

She stands, thinks, closes her eyes and lets her memory dance down the river towards an answer. "Oh, I don't know, doll," she says, eventually. "Should be around 80 now, I think? Maybe a little older?"

"You don't know?" I ask. She chortles at this.

"Oh, doll, I have received more minutes than I know what to do with. What's the point of keeping track of all that time passing, if you have so much more to spend?"

I glance at her display. There aren't more than a few years left on there. She catches my eye.

"Oh, I just had to buy myself another synthetic heart," she nods. "Took a decade and a half from me, the greedy bastards. But don't you worry!" she says, although I wasn't, "I'll have earned it back in no time. You don't cook like that in a city like this without getting rich in minutes." She chortles again.

A few other customers come in. She fills my glass up, and chats to the others for a long while. I don't mind. The pink, the food and the warmth have made me drowsy, and I listen in to other conversations, imagining what it would be like to live those people's lives. No one talks about time.

"8 Len," she says when I ask for the bill. I stare at her. 8 Len is a lot for a bowl of soup and two glasses of isodrink. Ten times what I would expect to pay. I shrug.

"I don't have any money," I say, "only minutes."

She studies me closely. "Y'know," she says, wiping her sweat on the pack of her hand and pinning down new strands of unruly hair, "normally, I take nine hours for a last meal." Someone gasps and double-checks the menu prices. "But I have a feeling this wasn't it for you. I can always tell."

"It was," I say and offer up my display.

"We'll see," she says. "Tell y'what. Gimme four hours."

"I'd be happy to pay nine –" I start, but she laughs and grasps my wrist.

"Oh, I know that," she says, and takes four hours. I thank her for the food and empty my glass before I leave. The city is awake now, and I have 1,813 minutes left.

I wonder what I was meant to be – a boy, a girl or a little bit of both. It has never really bothered me; there has been little room for it to bother me. But as I walk past people on the streets, grey bands, blue bands, the occasional yellow, I wonder how it would have been if I wasn't green banded. If my aptitude had been deemed somewhat less important, less grand. Would the void have found enough to eat, or would it have devoured me? I step into a tailor's shop. I negotiate with the owner, a grey band, who doesn't like taking minutes for payment, especially not from someone with so few minutes left. Eventually, we agree on products and price. He is reluctant, I can tell, but I smile and talk about unimportant things, and he eventually forgets.

"Are you a man or a woman?" he says when it comes

to fitting the chest area of the shirt I picked out. I shrug.

"Do you want high waist or low waist?"

"Low," I say.

"So wide top?" he says.

"No," I say.

"Narrow top, low waist, lace?"

"No lace."

"Tie?"

"Yes please."

He shakes his head and mumbles about youth today, and I smile and look at myself in the mirror. These will do well.

"Do you often make clothes for people to be buried in?" I ask.

"I don't know what people want to use my clothes for," he says, "I just sew." That makes sense, I guess.

"Are you sad I will be buried with these clothes?" I ask. Why not ask every question out loud? Why not?

"No," he says shortly. "Are you?"

I smile. "No. I'm glad I can afford to buy something nice for myself, so my family doesn't have to after I'm gone."

He nods, and we don't speak more after that.

1,489 minutes left. I walk until I hear the 1,440 chirp, and I smile and take a deep breath. I pass many baths on my way, but I know the type I'm looking for. I'm looking for one of the ones only gold bands can really afford. I've heard they do special deals for the dying.

"Did you bring clothes?" says the lady behind the counter. When I told her I was dying, she didn't even bat an eyelid. I found this reassuring.

"Yes," I say and hold out my box from the tailor. She nods.

"I'm sorry, I..." she says, looking me up and down. "Should I schedule you with a male or female attendant?"

"It doesn't matter," I say.

"No, you see... We have this policy... It has to be someone of the same sex as you."

"I'm neither, really," I say. "I promise."

She loses her smile, just for a second. "Nguvu will come and get you when he's ready," she smiles. She wants me. She chose to see the boy. "Please take a seat, and have some water." She hands me a glass of the clearest liquid I have ever seen. Pure water. I have never had any before. It tastes of fresh nothing; not the nothing of space in your mouth, but the nothing of wind and rainfall. It's very soothing. The taste of nothing. Two new tastes in a day.

Nguvu is a large black man. His muscles bulge and press against his clothes, and his smile is like a crack in the wall. He is beautiful. He bows down to me deeply, and I bow deeply back. We don't speak. He takes my bag of clothes and hands them to a young girl, who disappears behind a large door. I follow him through a labyrinth of corridors, all with illuminated walls that change colours as we pass. I relax.

He strips me of my clothes and leaves me standing in the middle of a small cubicle.

"Take a deep breath," he says, so I do. A second later I am dusted in gold. "Now, exhale." I do. He leads me by the hand to a small pool; we walk out into the middle. He scrubs me with his enormous hands and a series of coloured sponges. He pours warm water over my head and body, over and over. The water turns pale gold and winks at me. Nguvu leans me back onto his left arm and helps me relax. I don't float exactly; I feel heavy. He keeps my nose and mouth above water, but the rest of me is submerged for a long time. I breathe slowly, feel the water run along my body. It swishes gently by my ear, rustles my hair, and I think of nothing.

When I stand back up, the pool is clear again, and Nguvu starts soaping me, wrapping me in layers of foam and bubbles. It smells of something, but I don't know what. A new smell. It is nice, fresh, uplifting. It is also sweet. And dark.

The massage is slow and deep. Nguvu pushes down through my muscles, softens them, pushes them back into place. It makes me think of Mami demonstrating bread-baking in the museum when I was little. I used to sit with my legs crossed in front of the tourists and watch her knead and knead. I was so proud to have a Mami who knew how to perform such ancient arts. I would watch the faces of tourists eating freshly baked bread for the first time in their lives, the way their mouths moved to chew the tough grains, the way they stared admiringly at Mami. Mami is wonderful. I cry a little now, but it may be soap in my eyes.

As he digs through my muscles, I run through my memories. The void is hungry now; it starts tearing into anything I conjure up. The first day of green teachings, the way I wore a ribbon in my hair. The first time I won a competition and the council representative called me a fine young man. The first time someone called me beautiful. The night my parents danced on the kitchen floor, and the night I danced on the kitchen floor with Morvarid to prepare her for her first school dance. I smile and cry and feed the void bits of these memories I no longer need. I hope the void will disappear with me.

Nguvu dresses me in my new clothes, combs my hair and brushes gold dust on my cheeks and forehead. I see myself in the mirror, and I am an ancient God. I glow and issue commandments that stretch out over the remaining world and bring me silence.

They feed me clear water and grains, a piece of real fruit – the sweetest thing I've ever tasted. It's not much larger than my thumbnail, but it fills me with colours. M'ngo they call it, and the word spins in my head until I am dizzy. They leave me with an hour. That is the deal.

59 minutes left. I walk through the city, smiling at people I pass. It's almost time, and I'm ready. I try not to think too much about what will happen. When I was five or six years old, I witnessed a death with Zawadi. She was walking me home from a play date, and an old man came walking out of a house, locked the door behind him and waited patiently until a Timer drove up to him. They nodded to each other, and the Timer stuck his tally in under the man's chin. His chest opened. The Timer took out the gastro unit, and I screamed and screamed. Zawadi ran home and got Mami. Meanwhile, I watched the Timer empty the old man of recyclable parts, extract his tally and make sure the man closed up correctly.

Mami could not comfort me.

"He only ran out of time," she explained, trying to soothe me with hugs and kisses. "He was old. It was his time. They have to collect the gastro units so other children can be born, and live. We need them so we can eat, so we can take in food. You know this, Chi. You know this. Please. Tomodachi, please," she said, begging for me to calm down. I cried for days.

I'm starting to become a little stressed. I wonder if it will hurt, dying. They say it doesn't, but they say so many things. I walk quicker and try not to check my display too often. When there are finally ten minutes left, I can't wait any longer. I grab hold of the first Timer I see.

"Please," I say. "I have done what I can to make the time go faster. Can we just... get it over with?"

He looks at me, and then at my display. He shrugs and leads me to a bench nearby. We sit down a little awkwardly. I wonder if this is new protocol.

"Do you smoke?" he says, and offers me a cigarette from a packet he keeps in his breast pocket.

"No thank you, those things will kill you," I say. He laughs, and it takes me a couple of seconds to realise why. "...In a manner of speaking, I suppose," I say, suddenly shy. I accept a cigarette and try it. This one changes flavours every two drags. It's not too bad, but it stings a little on the way down. He checks my display with his tally.

"You have been busy," he says. Smokes. "Are you ready then?"

"For what?"

"Dying."

"Oh." I take a deep drag and hold the flavour in my mouth. I wish I hadn't accepted the cigarette. I wish I had let the M'ngo be the last thing I tasted. "Yeah."

"Seen it all?"

"What do you mean?"

"Seen the mountains? The cloud steps? The ocean?"

"Well, I haven't actually seen the ocean... not the *actual* ocean," I say. He smiles and looks at me.

"Everyone should see the ocean. You'd like it. It's beautiful."

This annoys me. "Well... I didn't," I say.

"Yeah... guess it's a bit late now..." he says, as if the situation is only now dawning on him.

"Yeah."

"Fuck," he says. I laugh. I haven't heard this word for ages. My auntie used to say it when she got really angry, but she hadn't for a long while now. It's such a misplaced old word on such a young man.

"What's it like?"

"Big," he says. "Very big. And violent. It looks... it looks like... it's just *more* than anything you will ever see. It doesn't have any lights or glow in it. And there are no controls or buttons. And it doesn't care if you have few or many minutes left. If you disappear in the ocean, you just have to stay there. It claims you. I think that's pretty neat. It's so hard to get lost today. Everyone is tracked, you know? But not in the ocean. It's kind, I think, it means you no harm. All your petty little things are just too insignificant for it to worry about, so it swallows them."

Like the void, I think.

"What?" he says.

"What?" I say.

"You said something."

"No I didn't."

He shrugs. We smoke.

"So… are you a… I mean, you look… are you…"

I shrug. "A little bit of both."

"Pretty," he says. I feel myself blushing. "I like you." I look down. "By the ocean, they have these frozen flavours. Hundreds of kinds, and you get them in these small bowls, one for each flavour. And you can walk around, tasting them all, looking at the ocean. It's great." He smiles.

"Oh," I say. I wish I had gone to the ocean. One minute left. He tosses his cigarette on the ground and it crumbles. My mouth tastes ashen.

"Are you ready, then?"

I'm not, but I nod. He gives me his hand and helps me to my feet. I shiver.

"Close your eyes," he says, and I do. I hold my breath. Ready for the sting.

He kisses me slowly. His lips are warm and soft, and nothing like I thought they would be. They make my cheeks burn and my fingers stretch for him. I stop them.

"I…" I say. I have been kissed before. By some girls who thought they saw a boy, and by some boys who thought they saw a girl. The void swallowed them all, and I didn't feel like either. But this one is different. He didn't kiss the girl, and he didn't kiss the boy. He didn't kiss one or the other, but a little bit of both. His kiss etches onto my lips and defines their outline. This is a good way to go. He connects to my display. I close my eyes. Swallow.

"There," he says. "Use them well."

"What?" I look down. 10,000 minutes left.

"What?" I say, and this time it comes out louder. Harsh. Cold. "I didn't even think you were allowed to give minutes to the dying. You're a Timer!" I say, or scream.

"Yeah, but not *your* Timer," he shrugs. I don't understand.

"I told you –" I begin. There is the briefest flash of annoyance across his face.

"Yeah, but that's not how it works," he says. "We get assigned to you. Someone would have been along in a minute or two, I'm sure, but you weren't assigned to me. I wouldn't be sitting here if you were. No one likes hanging around dying people. They're depressing."

"Wow, thanks..." I say. He doesn't reply, so I continue. "But I ran out of time..."

"Yes, but that doesn't mean anything until you're collected. It's a note on when you *should* die, not when you actually will. In the mountains, there are people who run out of time days before a Timer can get there. Plays real havoc with their funeral plans." He laughs at this, but I feel like screaming. He has given me almost a week's worth of Grade-A minutes. His kiss is still burning on my lips, and I feel like punching him, kissing him, crying against his shoulder.

"Please… take them back…" I am shivering. He shrugs.

"Nah," he says, "everyone should see the ocean."

We talk for a long time. He keeps his hand on my shoulder for a while, then we sit back down. He tells me about his brother who got his display removed, and I tell him about Morvarid and how she has become a pearl made of other people's years.

"Fuck," he says.

"Yeah," I smile. His tally beeps and he gets up.

"Good luck," he says. "If things change, come find me." He gives me a little note with his TIP-number. I put it in my pocket, but I know I won't use it. I still want to die. I just want to see the ocean first. I want to try frozen flavours and see if the ocean is anything like the void. I wonder if I should call home, tell them that I'll hang on for another week. But I don't.

"Excuse me," I say to the first transporter in the transpo-line. "I will pay you six days if you can take me to the ocean."

"Six days?" he says. He is a rather old man with a thick moustache. He has beads and prayer wheels on the dashboard and he smiles the way my father smiles: big, with eyes. "It's only a few hours' drive away! Six days is too much. Five hours. Come on in! Come in!"

"No," I say, "I have to be allowed to pay you six days."

"Sure, sure, crazy gir– hmm… No. Crazy one, come in!" he says, and he zaps up into the second layer and shuffles in between two other cars with a speed and accuracy that terrifies me.

"Why, crazy one, are you going to the sea?" he says when he's successfully navigated into the fast field and gotten us out of the city. I've never been this far east before. The landscape is different.

"I've never seen it before," I say.

"What?" he says, and goes through a whole little pantomime of surprise, slapping his thigh, shaking his head, snapping his fingers. "You are too old not to have seen the ocean! You must be, what, at least 20!"

"22."

"Too old, about time."

"I'm dying," I say.

"We are all dying."

"Yes, but I am dying in a week."

He looks at me in the mirror but doesn't answer. He makes couple of jerks over in the next field, bypassing an old lady and a Timer-patrol.

"I am dying soon too," he says. "Maybe a month. Maybe more. It depends how much I can work." I can see his display from where I'm sitting. I stare. To me, it looks like he has abut 80 years left. But that's impossible. He must be 70, at least. "I have been saving," he says, jiggling his display to show me the numbers. "Driving taxi all day and all night, only home on the last day, maybe, and never been ill or on holiday."

"What are you saving for?"

"Shuttle space," he says. I nod. The time price for a ticket now is about 85 years, or so I've heard.

"But..." I say, "it will take you at least ten years to get there."

He laughs. "I do not want to get there. I am a transporter. I have transported people all around the planet, seen it from a little above. But, crazy one, I have never seen the transporters from above. And I would like to. I think we would look small…" He goes quiet, for a long time.

"Besides," he says, when I have almost fallen asleep from the heat and the slow humming of the car. "They cannot get me, out there."

"Who can't?"

"The Timers. I don't want to be recycled. It's selfish, perhaps. But I worry it will hurt… I saw someone being recycled once, and after they were finished, he still blinked. His eyes were so big and his mouth was opening and closing. It took at least a minute before his eyes were still. I don't want to be that man." I shiver. I remember the eyes of the man I saw, eye shifting, mouth opening and closing. "I just want my minutes to run out, and that be that."

"The minutes don't actually matter," I say.

"I guess not," he says, somewhere else completely.

"No, I mean… in the mountains, sometimes the Timers don't find you for days, and people just go on living without minutes left."

He thinks about this. "You don't say," he says. "You don't say." We ride in silence until the landscape opens up into endless motion, and our car starts shaking slightly. I try to lock eyes with the motion, but it shifts and changes, sometimes white, sometimes green; sometimes it ripples, sometimes it turns or churns beneath me. I cannot breathe.

"What do you think, crazy one?" he says. I see his eyes in the mirror, and he is laughing.

"Is this the ocean?" I whisper.

"Yes, of course."

The ocean is nothing like the void.

He drops me off at a small village. I reach out my display to pay, and then stop.

"Do you know how much frozen flavours cost in time?"

"A minute per flavour, I believe," he says, "at least they used to."

"Okay…" I say, and reach my arm forward again. I stop. "Do you think they have mushrooms here?"

"Maybe," he nods. "Many places do in the countryside."

"Are they expensive?"

"Not very." His eyes are dancing and his moustache is quivering; his entire face is made of laughter and I don't get the joke. I stretch my hand out again. "You still sure you want me to take six days?"

"Yes," I say, and he shrugs.

"There," he says after taking his payment. I don't want to look. "Enjoy yourself!" he calls after me, but I don't turn back.

I walk in silvery sand and watch my footsteps become shapes in the water, reappear and reform, over and over. I buy every single frozen flavour, and eat them one by one. One tastes like M'ngo, and I wish I could tell someone. The man who works in the café laughs when I ask for mushrooms.

"Of course," he says. "How do you want them?" so

I buy them three ways. Then, and only then, do I check my minutes. I should have about three hours left, and I would like to see some more of the ocean before I die. I have six days. More.

I sit in the silver sand for a long while, watching the water slip in and out of now and then, and I think about what the Timer said, about how it swallows everything. I think about letting it swallow me. Walking until I slip down through its wet teeth and disappear beneath its tongue. It is tiring to wait for death, and I decide to sleep in the sand tonight. The sound of the ocean is soothing. It's loud.

My pocket holds a small piece of card, and I turn it over and over between my fingers, reading his TIP-number a hundred times. There was a com caller back at the café.

The connection sound lasts forever.

"Hey," I say, "It's me. Eh... it's Tomodachi."

We have so much to talk about, but we can't find the words. I mostly cry.

"Mami," I say. "I'm in a village by Kodochu. Maybe you and the others could come and spend a day or two with me... if you have the time."

They do.